MASTER DETECTIVE

Astrid Lindgren

Translated by Susan Beard

OXFORD
UNIVERSITY PRESS

BLOOD! NO DOUBT ABOUT IT!

He stared at the red stain through the magnifying glass. Then he moved his pipe from one side of his mouth to the other and sighed. Of course it was blood. What else usually came out when you cut your thumb? That stain *should* have been the final proof that Sir Henry had bumped off his wife in one of the most gruesome murders any detective would have to solve. But unfortunately—it wasn't! The sad truth was that his knife had slipped while he was sharpening his pencil. And naturally Sir Henry wasn't responsible for that. Especially since Sir Henry, the chump, didn't even exist. Unfair, that's what it was! Why were some people lucky enough to be born in the rough streets of London or the ganglands of Chicago, where murder and shootings were part of everyday life? While, as for him . . . ! Reluctantly he took his eyes off the blood stain and looked out of the window instead.

In absolute peace and tranquillity the High Street lay

dozing in the summer sunshine.

The chestnut trees were in flower. There was not a living thing to be seen apart from the baker's grey cat sitting on the pavement, licking its paws. Not even the most highly-trained detective's eye could observe anything to suggest a crime had been committed. It was truly hopeless being a super-sleuth in this town! When he grew up he would take himself off to London as soon as he had the chance. Or perhaps he should go to Chicago instead? His dad wanted him to start work in their shop. The shop! Him! Oh, they'd love that, all those murderers and gangsters in London and Chicago! They would be free to commit murder all over the place with no one to stop them, while he would be standing in the shop wrapping cheese and weighing up sugar and macaroni. Oh no, he had no intention of being a salami-slicer. Detective, or nothing at all. His dad would have to choose! Sherlock Holmes, Lord Peter Wimsey, Hercule Poirot, Kalle Blomkvist! And he, Kalle Blomkvist, planned to be the best of them all.

'Blood! No doubt about it,' he muttered proudly.

There was a thumping on the staircase. Seconds later his door flew open and there stood Anders, hot and out of breath. Kalle studied him closely and drew his conclusions.

'You've been running,' he stated.

'Of course I've been running,' said Anders, irritably. 'Do you think I floated in on a magic carpet?'

Kalle hid his pipe. Not that it mattered to him if Anders thought he was smoking in secret, it was just that there was no tobacco in his pipe. But a detective needs his pipe when he is wrestling with tricky problems, even if he has temporarily run out of tobacco.

'Are you coming out?' asked Anders, and he threw himself onto Kalle's bed.

Kalle nodded. Of course he wanted to go out! He had to do his evening street patrol anyway, just *in case* anything suspicious had come up. Yes, there were policemen, but everyone knew what they were like. They wouldn't recognize a murderer if they tripped over one.

Kalle put his magnifying glass into his desk drawer and then he and Anders thundered down the stairs, making the house shake to its foundations.

'Kalle! Don't forget you've got to water the strawberry patch this evening!'

That was Kalle's mother, with her head poked round the kitchen door.

Kalle gave her a casual wave. Of course he would water the strawberries! Later on. Just as soon as he had convinced himself there were no shifty individuals lurking about the town with their minds set on trouble. Not that the chances were great, unfortunately, but you should never be caught off guard. He had seen the result of that in the Buxton Case. There they were, having a quiet stroll, when bam! Shots in the night and four murders before you had time to blink. That's what the villains had been counting on. No one would have suspected it in such a small town on such a lovely summer's day. But they didn't know Kalle Blomkvist!

On the ground floor was the shop. *Viktor Blomkvist, Grocer*, the sign said.

'Ask your dad for some sweets,' said Anders.

Kalle had already thought of that. He stuck his head through the doorway. There behind the counter stood *Viktor Blomkvist, Grocer*, the very man. His dad, in other words.

'Dad, I'll just take a few of these stripy ones!'

Viktor Blomkvist, Grocer, threw a loving look at his fair-haired offspring and grunted good-naturedly. Kalle dipped his hand into the sweet jar. The grunt meant he could help himself. Then he quickly went back to Anders who was sitting on the swing under the pear tree, waiting. But Anders wasn't interested in the stripy ones at that very moment. He was staring with an idiotic expression on his face at something in the baker's garden. The something was the baker's little Eva-Lotta. She was sitting on her swing wearing a red-checked dress. She was swinging to and fro and eating a bun. She was singing, too, because she was a girl of many talents.

'*A sailor went to sea, sea, sea to see what he could see, see, see . . .*'

She had a high, clear voice which carried perfectly

across to Kalle and Anders. Kalle gazed longingly at Eva-Lotta as he distractedly offered Anders a sweet. Anders took one, equally distractedly, as he stared equally longingly at Eva-Lotta. Kalle sighed. He absolutely adored Eva-Lotta. So did Anders. Kalle had made up his mind to marry Eva-Lotta, as soon as he had made enough money for somewhere to live. So had Anders. But Kalle was sure she would prefer him, Kalle. A detective with, let's say, forty solved murder cases under his belt. That had to impress her more than a train driver. A train driver—that was what Anders wanted to be.

Eva-Lotta swung and sang and looked as if she didn't have the faintest idea that she was being watched.

'Eva-Lotta!' called Kalle.

' . . . but all that he could see, see, see was the bottom of the deep blue sea, sea, sea,' continued Eva-Lotta.

'Eva-Lotta!' shouted Kalle and Anders together.

'Oh, is it you?' said Eva-Lotta, looking surprised. She jumped off the swing and obligingly walked up to the fence that separated her garden from Kalle's. There was a plank missing. Kalle had taken it away himself, an excellent arrangement which made it possible to chat easily through the opening and even squeeze their way into the baker's garden without having to take any roundabout routes. Anders was secretly annoyed that Kalle lived so close to Eva-Lotta. It was unfair, somehow. He lived far away in a different street, where he and his parents and his little brothers and sisters lived crammed into one room and a kitchen above his father's shoemaker's shop.

'Coming for a wander around town with us, Eva-Lotta?' asked Kalle.

Eva-Lotta enjoyed the last mouthful of her bun.

'Could do,' she said. She brushed a crumb from her dress, and off they went.

It was Saturday. Fredrik the Foot was drunk already and standing outside the tannery as usual, with a circle of onlookers around him. Kalle and Anders and Eva-Lotta joined them to listen while Fredrik told stories about his heroic deeds from when he was building the railways up in Norrland.

As Kalle listened, his eyes scanned the crowd. Not for a second had he forgotten his duty. Anything suspicious? No, he had to admit, there was nothing suspicious, although he had heard that when things looked innocent they could be quite the opposite. Best to be on his guard! Toiling up the road, for example, was a man with a sack on his back.

'What if,' Kalle said, giving Anders a nudge, 'What if that sack is full of stolen silver!'

'What if it isn't?' answered Anders impatiently, because he wanted to listen to Fredrik the Foot. 'What if you go completely crackers one of these days with all your detective stuff?'

Eva-Lotta laughed. Kalle kept quiet. He was used to

being misunderstood.

Eventually the police turned up, as expected, and took Fredrik the Foot away. He usually spent Saturday night in the local jail.

'You took your time,' complained Fredrik the Foot, as Constable Björk grabbed his arm. 'I've been waiting over an hour for you. Got your work cut out chasing all the villains in this town, have you?'

Constable Björk smiled and showed his perfect white teeth.

'Come on, let's be having you,' he said.

The group of onlookers dispersed, and Kalle and Anders and Eva-Lotta walked slowly away. They had really wanted to hear more of Fredrik the Foot's stories.

'Look how pretty the chestnut trees are,' said Eva-Lotta, gazing at the long row of trees lining the High Street.

'Yes, the flowers look nice,' said Anders. 'Like candles.'

Everywhere was calm and quiet. You could practically feel it would soon be Sunday. Here and there they could see people eating dinner in their gardens. They had already washed off the working week and were sitting in their best clothes, ready for the weekend. They chatted and laughed and looked as if they were having a fine old time under their fruit trees, which were full of blossom. Kalle and Anders and Eva-Lotta looked long and hard over every garden gate as they walked past. If they were in luck a kind person might offer them a tasty snack. But it didn't look like that was going to happen.

'We've got to find something to do,' said Eva-Lotta.

Just then they heard the sharp whistle of a train in the distance.

'Here comes the 7 o'clock,' said Anders.

'I know what,' said Kalle. 'We can hide behind the lilac hedge in Eva-Lotta's garden with a parcel tied to a string. When someone walks past and finds the parcel, we can pull the string and see what they do.'

'Yes, that sounds like a suitable occupation for a Saturday evening,' said Anders.

Eva-Lotta didn't say anything, but she nodded in approval.

They soon had a parcel made. After all, everything they needed could be found in Viktor Blomkvist's grocer's shop.

'It looks as if there's something very nice inside,' said Eva-Lotta proudly.

'Yes, and let's see who takes the bait,' said Anders.

The parcel lay there on the pavement, looking very interesting and tempting. You couldn't tell at first glance that it was attached to a piece of string, and that the string disappeared behind the baker's lilac bushes. An observant passer-by might of course have heard a certain amount of giggling and whispering coming from behind the hedge. However, Mrs Petronella Apelgren, proprietor of the town's largest butcher's shop, who was at that very minute walking down the street, was not paying enough attention to hear or see anything suspicious. But she saw the parcel. With rather of lot of effort she bent over to pick it up.

'Pull!' whispered Anders to Kalle, who was holding the string.

And Kalle pulled. At startling speed the parcel disappeared behind the lilac hedge. This time Mrs Apelgren couldn't avoid hearing the muffled laughter. She let fly with a stream of abuse. The children couldn't quite make out everything she said, but several times they heard her mention the words 'young offenders' institution' as a suitable place to send unruly children.

Behind the hedge it was now deathly quiet. After firing off a final round of complaints, Mrs Apelgren walked away, still booming in indignation.

'That was fun,' said Eve-Lotta. 'I wonder who'll come along next. I hope it's someone who gets as angry as she did.'

But it seemed as if the town had gone stone dead all of a sudden. No one came along, and the three friends behind the hedge had almost made up their minds to give up the whole idea when Anders whispered:

'No, wait, someone's coming after all.'

And someone was coming. He swung round the corner and headed rapidly towards the baker's front gate, a tall figure in a grey suit, no hat, and a large suitcase in one hand.

'Get ready,' whispered Anders, when the man stopped in front of the parcel.

Kalle got ready, but it was no good. They heard the man give a low whistle, and the next second he put his foot down on the parcel.

2

'And what's your name, my pretty young lady?' asked the man a moment later, when Eva-Lotta and her two companions crawled out from behind the hedge.

'Eve-Lotta Lisander,' said Eva-Lotta, confidently.

'Just as I thought,' said the man. 'We go back a long way, you and me. I saw you when you were small enough to fit a cradle and scream and be sick and carry on all day.'

Eva-Lotta tossed her head. She couldn't believe she had ever been that small.

'How old are you now?' asked the man.

'Thirteen,' said Eva-Lotta.

'Thirteen! And you've got two boyfriends already! One fair-haired, one dark. You like a bit of variety, that's for sure,' the man said, with an annoying grin.

Eva-Lotta tossed her head again. She didn't have to stand here taking insults from someone she didn't know.

'And who are you?' she asked, thinking to herself that whoever he was, he had probably been sick as a baby, too.

'Me? I'm Uncle Einar, my dear. Your mother's cousin!'
He pulled one of Eva-Lotta's blonde curls.

'And what are your boyfriends called, by the way?'

Eva-Lotta introduced Anders and Kalle, and one dark and one fair head nodded politely.

'What nice boys,' said Uncle Einar, approvingly. 'But don't go marrying them! Marry me instead,' he went on, laughing. His laugh sounded just like a horse. 'I'll build you a mansion and you can spend all day doing whatever you like.'

'You're too old for me, Uncle,' said Eva-Lotta bluntly.

Anders and Kalle felt a little left out of the conversation. Who was this lanky idiot who had turned up out of the blue?

'Description. Let me see,' Kalle said to himself. It was a matter of principle for him to make a mental note of the appearance of every unknown person he came across. Who could tell—they might not all be honest, decent people!

'Description: brown combed-back hair, brown eyes, eyebrows that meet in the middle, straight nose, sticky-out teeth, square jaw, grey suit, brown shoes, no hat, brown suitcase, goes by the name of Uncle Einar.' That was about it. No, hang on. Of course, there was a small red scar on one cheek.

Kalle mentally stored every detail.

'And extremely annoying,' he added, to himself.

'Is your Mum at home, my little pumpkin?' asked Uncle Einar.

'Yes. Here she comes now.'

Eva-Lotta pointed to the woman who was walking down the garden path. As she came closer it was clear she had the same cheerful blue eyes as Eva-Lotta.

'Do I have the pleasure of being recognized?' Uncle Einar bowed.

'Gracious me. Is it you, Einar? It's been ages since we last saw you. Where did you suddenly spring from?'

Mrs Lisander's eyes were wide open in surprise.

'The moon,' said Uncle Einar. 'To cheer you up in your quiet little corner of the world!'

'Obviously he didn't come from the moon,' said Eva-Lotta. 'He came on the seven o'clock train.'

'Same old joker,' said Mrs Lisander. 'But why didn't you write and let us know you were coming?'

'My dear girl, never put in writing what you can say in person, that's my philosophy. You know me, I'm the kind of person who acts on impulse. I thought it might be nice to have a little holiday and suddenly I recalled that I have a particularly nice cousin who lives in a particularly nice little town. So, may I stay?'

Mrs Lisander thought fast. It wasn't easy to take someone in on the spur of the moment. Oh well, he could have the room at the end of the house.

'And what a delightful daughter you've got,' said Uncle

Einar, and he pinched Eva-Lotta's cheek.

'Ouch, get off,' said Eva-Lotta. 'That hurts!'

'It was meant to,' said Uncle Einar.

'Of course you are welcome,' said Mrs Lisander. 'How long is your holiday?'

'Ah, well, I'm not entirely sure. To be honest, I've decided to leave the business. I'm considering moving abroad. There's no future in this country. Nothing ever moves here. It just marches up and down on the same old spot.'

'No it doesn't!' said Eva-Lotta vehemently. 'This is the best country ever.'

Uncle Einar put his head on one side and looked at Eva-Lotta.

'How you have grown, little Eva-Lotta,' he said, and once again he neighed his horse-like laugh, which Eva-Lotta was starting to detest with a vengeance.

'The boys can help me with this,' said Mrs Lisander, nodding at the suitcase.

'Negative! I prefer to take it myself,' Uncle Einar said.

That night Kalle was woken by a mosquito biting his forehead. And seeing as he was awake he might as well check to see if there were any gangsters or robbers getting up to their tricks in the area. First he looked out of the window facing the High Street. All was deserted. Then he peered out from behind the curtain in the other window which overlooked the baker's back garden. There was the baker's house, dark and sleeping among the apple blossom. The only light came from a room at the end of the house. And silhouetted against the blind was the dark shadow of a man.

'Ugh, that Uncle Einar. What an absolute idiot,' said Kalle to himself.

The shadow moved to and fro, to and fro. What a restless soul he was, that Uncle Einar!

Why is he wandering about like that? thought Kalle, and then he leapt back into his own comfy bed.

It was hardly eight o'clock on Monday morning when he heard Anders give a whistle outside the window. He, Kalle and Eva-Lotta had their own signal.

Kalle threw on his clothes. A brand new day of the school holidays lay before him, with no problems, no school and no other duties apart from watering the strawberry patch and keeping an eye out for potential murderers in the neighbourhood. Neither of which was especially demanding.

It was a brilliantly sunny day. Kalle drank a glass of milk, ate some toast and raced to the door before his mother had time to issue even half the instructions she had intended giving him along with his breakfast.

Now all they had to do was get Eva-Lotta to come out.

For some reason, Kalle and Anders didn't feel right asking her directly. Strictly speaking, it wasn't even quite right to play with girls. But it couldn't be helped. Everything was much more fun when she was with them. And anyhow, she wasn't the kind to hold back when there was some fun to be had. She was as daring and quick as any boy. When the water tower was being repaired she had climbed up the scaffolding as high as Anders and Kalle, and when Constable Björk spotted their prank and told them it would be best if they left immediately, she sat down calmly at the very end of a plank, which would have given anyone else vertigo, and laughed:

'Come up and get us!'

She probably hadn't expected Constable Björk to take her literally. But Constable Björk was the best gymnast in the town's gymnastics team, and it didn't take him many seconds to climb up to Eva-Lotta.

'Ask your dad to get you a trapeze,' he said. 'Because at least if you fall off that there's a chance you won't break your neck!' Then he took a tight hold of Eva-Lotta and climbed down with her. Anders and Kalle had managed to clamber down to the ground with remarkable speed. Ever since then they had liked Constable Björk. And liked Eva-Lotta as well, of course, quite apart from the fact that they both planned to marry her.

'It was brave of her to speak like that to a police officer,' said Anders. 'Not many girls would have done that. Not many boys either, come to think of it.'

And what about that misty autumn evening when they had played a joke with a whoopee cushion on that miserable old bank cashier who was always so cruel to his dog? Eva-Lotta stood under his window and parped and parped until the bank cashier came running out and almost caught her red-handed. But Eva-Lotta had hopped swiftly over the fence and disappeared down Båtmansgatan, where Anders and Kalle were waiting for her.

No, there was nothing wrong with Eva-Lotta. Kalle and Anders were agreed on that. Anders gave another of his whistles, in the hope Eva-Lotta would hear. And she did. Eva-Lotta came out, but two steps behind came Uncle Einar.

'Can this little lad join in your games?' he said.

Anders and Kalle looked at him with embarrassment.

'Hide-and-seek, what about that?' neighed Uncle Einar. 'I want to be the one who hides!'

'Urgh,' said Eva-Lotta.

'Or what about going to look at the castle ruins?' suggested Uncle Einar. 'They are still there, aren't they?'

Naturally the castle ruins were still there. After all, they were the town's greatest attraction, one that every visitor had to see even before they looked at the painted ceiling in the church. Not that there were many tourists. The ruins were perched on a hilltop, looking down over the little town. An important nobleman had built the castle in the old days and eventually a town had grown up around it. The small town was still busy and thriving, but not much remained of the castle apart from the beautiful ruins.

Kalle and Anders and Eva-Lotta had nothing against visiting the old ruins. It was one of their favourite places. You could play hide-and-seek in the old rooms or defend the tower from invading troops.

Uncle Einar walked quickly up the narrow track that wound its way up to the ruins. Kalle, Anders and Eva-Lotta tagged after him. From time to time they caught each other's eye and winked knowingly.

'I'd like to give him a bucket and spade so he can sit and play on his own somewhere,' whispered Anders.

'And you reckon that's what he would do?' said Kalle. 'Oh no, when grown-ups decide they want to play with children, nothing can stop them, believe me!'

'They want to be entertained, that's the problem,' said Eva-Lotta, in a superior tone. 'But seeing as he's Mum's cousin we'd better try and entertain him, otherwise he'll get tricky.'

'That won't be easy if he's planning a very *long* holiday,' said Anders.

'Oh, he'll be going abroad soon,' said Eva-Lotta. 'You heard him. This is no country to live in.'

'Well, I for one won't shed any tears when he's gone,' said Kalle.

Wild roses bloomed on tangled briars around the old ruins. Bees buzzed and the air shimmered in the heat. But inside the ruins it was cool. Uncle Einar looked around with interest.

'It's a pity you can't go down into the cellar,' said Anders.

'And why can't you?' asked Uncle Einar.

'Because they've blocked it off with a heavy door,' said Kalle. 'And it's kept locked. There are supposed to be tunnels and dungeons down there, but it's wet and damp so they don't want people going in. The mayor keeps the key.'

'People used to trip over and break their legs down there,' said Anders. 'And one kid almost got lost. So now no one can go in. But it's a real shame, because you could have a lot of fun in there.'

'Do you really want to go down there?' asked Uncle Einar. 'Because I might be able to arrange it.'

'How would that work?' asked Eva-Lotta.

'Like this,' said Uncle Einar, and he took a little gadget from his pocket. He fiddled with the lock for a moment and then the door groaned on its hinges.

The children stared in astonishment; first at Uncle Einar and then at the door. This was pure magic.

'How did you do it, Uncle Einar? Can I have a look at that thing?' asked Kalle eagerly.

Uncle Einar held out the small metal object.

'Is it—is it a lock pick?'

'Correct,' said Uncle Einar.

Kalle was thrilled. He had read a lot about lock picks but he had never seen one.

'Can I hold it?' he asked. He was handed the lock pick and felt this was a momentous occasion in his life. Then a thought struck him. According to the books, it was generally only shady characters who went around with lock picks. This called for an explanation.

'Why exactly have you got a lock pick, Uncle Einar?' he asked.

'Because I don't like locked doors,' answered uncle Einar sharply.

'Aren't we going down?' said Eva-Lotta. 'And there's nothing special about lock picks,' she added, as if she had done nothing but pick locks all her life.

Anders was already half-way down the rickety staircase that led to the cellar. His brown eyes shone with the prospect of adventure. This was exciting. Only Kalle thought a lock pick was something special. Old dungeons, on the other hand—now that was really something! With a little imagination you could almost hear the rattle of chains that had held the poor prisoners captive here hundreds of years before.

'I hope the place isn't haunted,' said Eva-Lotta, casting anxious looks to right and left as she climbed down the stairs.

'Don't be too sure,' said Uncle Einar. 'What if a grisly old ghost came and pinched you. Like this!'

'Ow!' shrieked Eva-Lotta. 'Stop pinching! I'll get a bruise on that arm now, I know it.'

Angrily, she rubbed her arm.

Anders and Kalle nosed around everywhere like two bloodhounds.

'Think if you could come down here as often as you wanted!' said Anders in amazement. 'And map it all out. And have it as your hideaway.'

He stared into the dark passageways that branched out in all directions.

'They could search for you here for two whole weeks without so much as a clue. If you had hurt someone and needed to hide, this dungeon would be a perfect hideaway.'

'You don't say,' said Uncle Einar.

Kalle walked around with his nose almost touching the ground.

'What on earth are you doing?' asked Uncle Einar.

Kalle blushed.

'I was just looking to see if there was any trace of those poor blighters who were kept prisoner here.'

'Honestly, there have been hundreds of people in here since then, you twit,' said Eva-Lotta.

'Perhaps you don't know that Kalle is a detective, Uncle Einar?' Anders sounded rather amused and superior as he said it.

'Blow me down, I had no idea,' said Uncle Einar.

'Oh yes. One of the best there is, currently.'

Kalle glared fiercely at Anders.

'I certainly am not,' he said. 'But I enjoy thinking about that sort of thing. You know, criminals getting caught and such like. Nothing wrong with that, is there?'

'Absolutely not, my lad! I hope you soon round up a whole gang of rogues you can take to the police.'

Uncle Einar neighed. Kalle was fuming inside. Nobody took him seriously.

'No worries there,' said Anders. 'The worst thing to happen in this town was when Fredrik the Foot sneaked into the church vestry and pinched the collection money. Which, by the way, he returned the following day, once he had sobered up.'

'And now he's always in a cell over the weekend, so he won't be doing that again,' laughed Eva-Lotta.

'Otherwise you could have waited for him, Kalle, and caught him red-handed next time,' said Anders. 'Then at least you would have caught one villain.'

'Now you mustn't be unkind to the master detective here,' said Uncle Einar. One of these days he'll come up trumps and catch someone who's made off with a bar of chocolate from his dad's shop.'

Kalle was steaming angry. Anders and Eva-Lotta might possibly be allowed to joke with him, but no-one else, least of all that grinning Uncle Einar.

'Well, little Kalle,' said Uncle Einar. 'No doubt you'll be very good at it by the time you're finished! No, stop that!'

That last remark was directed at Anders, who had found a stump of pencil and was about to write his name on a smooth piece of stone wall.

'Why?' asked Eva-Lotta. 'Let us write our names and the date. It would be fun. We might come here again when we're really, really old, twenty-five or thereabouts. Then it would be fun to find our names here, wouldn't it?'

'Yes, it would remind us of our lost youth,' said Anders.

'Oh, well, do what you want,' said Uncle Einar.

Kalle was sulking and at first he didn't want to write his name, but he changed his mind and soon all three names stood in a neat row: Eva-Lotta Lisander, Anders Bengtsson and Kalle Blomkvist.

'Aren't you going to write your name too, Uncle?' Eva-Lotta asked Uncle Einar.

'I can most definitely assure you that I'm not,' said Uncle Einar. 'And anyway, it's very cold and damp down here, and not good for my old joints. Come on, let's go out in the sunshine again. Oh, and just one more thing,' he continued, as the door slammed shut behind them. 'We *haven't* been here, understood? No telling!'

'And why exactly mustn't we tell?' asked Eva-Lotta crossly.

'Well, young lady, that is a state secret,' said Uncle

Einar. 'And don't you forget it! Otherwise I'll pinch you again.'

'You just try,' said Eva-Lotta.

The sunlight dazzled them as they made their way out of the murky vaults, and the heat felt almost overwhelming.

'What if I try to make myself a bit more popular?' said Uncle Einar. 'How about fizzy drinks and cream cakes in the café gardens?'

Eva-Lotta nodded graciously.

'At times, Uncle, you come up with such good ideas.'

They found a table next to the low wall above the river bank. You could sit there and throw cake crumbs to the small fish that swam up hungrily and bobbed about just under the surface. Some tall lime trees offered cool shade, and when Uncle Einar ordered a plateful of cakes and three bottles of lemonade, even Kalle began to find his presence in town almost bearable.

Uncle Einar tipped back his chair, threw a few crumbs to the fish, drummed his fingers on the table and whistled a little melody. Then he said:

'Eat as much as you can, but be quick about it! We can't sit here all day.'

He's very odd, thought Kalle. He never wants to do one thing for very long.

'He became more and more convinced that Uncle Einar had a very restless disposition. Personally, he could sit here in the café garden all day, enjoying the cakes and the funny small fish and the sunshine. He couldn't understand why anyone would be in a hurry to leave.

Uncle Einar looked at his watch.

'Well, I suppose the Stockholm newspapers have arrived by now,' he said eagerly. 'Kalle, you're young and fit, run to the kiosk and buy one for me!'

Naturally, it has to be me who does the running about, thought Kalle.

'Anders is considerably younger and faster than I am,' he said.

'Really?'

'Yes, he was born five days after me. But then he's not so keen to help,' said Kalle, catching the one-krona coin that Uncle Einar tossed to him.

'Well, at least I can sneak a look at the paper,' he said to himself, after he had bought a copy at the kiosk. 'The headlines, at least. And the comic strips.'

It was full of the same old things, more or less. First a lot about financial matters and columns of political stuff that could be of no interest to anyone, then *Bus collides with train, Rats attack old man* and *Angry cow causes panic, Massive jewellery robbery* and *Why such high taxes?* Nothing particularly exciting, thought Kalle.

But Uncle Einar grabbed the newspaper eagerly. He leafed through it rapidly until he came to the page with the latest news. He became so engrossed in one article that he didn't hear when Eva-Lotta asked if she could help herself to another cake.

'What he's so interested in?' wondered Kalle. He very much wanted to stand behind Uncle Einar's shoulder and look, but he wasn't sure if Uncle Einar would take kindly to that. Evidently there was only one item he was reading, because he soon put the paper down and didn't bother taking it when they left the café garden shortly afterwards.

On the High Street they passed Constable Björk on his beat.

'Hello, Constable Björk,' shouted Eva-Lotta.

'Well, hello there,' said the constable, and saluted. 'I see you haven't fallen down and killed yourself yet.'

'Not yet,' answered Eva-Lotta. 'But tomorrow I intend climbing the viewing tower in the park, so there's still a chance. Unless you come and get me down, of course.'

'I suppose I'll have to make the effort,' said Constable Björk, and saluted again.

Uncle Einar grabbed Eva-Lotta's ear.

'You have close connections to the police force, I see,' he said.

'Ouch. Let go,' said Eva-Lotta. 'And isn't he so dreamy you could die?'

'Who, me?'

'Yuck,' said Eva-Lotta. 'Constable Björk, I mean.'

Outside the hardware shop, Uncle Einar came to a halt.

'Farewell, kids,' he said. 'I'm going in here for a while.'

'Good,' said Eva-Lotta, when he had disappeared.

'I agree. Even if he buys us cakes, nothing much can happen while he's hanging around,' said Anders.

Then Anders and Eva-Lotta amused themselves by standing on the bridge and seeing who could spit the furthest into the river. Kalle didn't take part. He had a sudden idea that he wanted to see what Uncle Einar was buying in the hardware shop. 'Purely routine,' he said to himself. But you can tell a great deal about a person from what they buy in a hardware shop. If he buys an iron, thought Kalle, then he is the domestic type, and if he buys a toboggan—well, if he buys one of those he's an absolute crackpot! With the current absence of snow he certainly wouldn't have much use for it. But I'm dead certain a toboggan is not what he's looking for!

Kalle stood by the shop window and peered in. There inside was Uncle Einar. The assistant was in the process of showing him something. Kalle shaded his eyes and tried to make out what it was. It was—it was a torch!

Kalle's brain whirred. *What* did Uncle Einar want a torch for? In the middle of the summer, when it was light all night! First a lock pick, now a torch. What was this, if not highly mysterious? Uncle Einar was a highly mysterious person, Kalle decided. And he,

Kalle Blomkvist, was not the type to let mysterious people wander about unchecked. Uncle Einar would immediately be put under Kalle Blomkvist's special surveillance.

Suddenly a thought struck him. The newspaper! When a mysterious person is so enormously interested in something in the newspaper, then that is mysterious too and should be examined closely. Purely routine!

He ran back to the café garden. The newspaper was still there on the table. Kalle picked it up and stuffed it inside his shirt. It would be saved for future reading. Even if *at the moment* he couldn't work out what Uncle Einar had been reading so intently, it might perhaps provide a few clues later on.

Master Detective Blomkvist walked home and watered the strawberries, very satisfied with himself.

'Something has got to be done,' said Anders. 'We can't hang around like this all summer. What can we *do*?'

He ran his hands through his thick black hair and looked as if he was racking his brains.

'One krona to anyone who comes up with plan,' said Eva-Lotta.

'A circus,' said Kalle slowly. 'What if we do a circus?'

Eva-Lotta jumped down from the swing.

'The krona is yours! Let's start this very minute!'

'But where shall we have it?' asked Anders.

'It'll have to be in our garden,' decided Eva-Lotta. 'Where else?'

It was true, the baker's garden was suitable for almost everything, so why not for a circus? The front garden was neat and tidy, with colourful flower beds and raked gravel paths. But the back garden, which sloped gently down to the river, was left to look after itself. It was an ideal place for all kinds of games. There was a flat area with short grass, suitable for football and croquet and athletics of various kinds. It was close to the bakery. There was always a wonderful smell of freshly-baked bread hovering over this part of the garden, and it blended deliciously with the fragrance of the lilac bushes. If you tried your hardest to keep as near to the bakery as you could, Eva-Lotta's dad might on occasion stick his head out of the window and ask if anyone would like a cinnamon bun or a Danish pastry. Further down towards the river bank grew a couple of ancient elm trees, which were excellent for climbing. It was quite easy to get to the top and from up there you had a terrific view over the whole town. You could see the river winding its way like a silver ribbon between the old houses and gardens. You could also see the ancient wooden church and, in the distance, the hill with the castle ruins.

The river formed a natural boundary for the baker's garden. A knobbly elm tree hung low over the water here, and its trunk was perfect for sitting on and fishing. Eva-Lotta and Anders and Kalle did that a lot, although naturally Eva-Lotta always grabbed the best place to sit.

'The circus must be next to the bakery,' said Eva-Lotta. 'Round the corner!'

Kalle and Anders nodded in agreement.

'We'll have to borrow tarpaulins,' said Anders. 'And we've got to put up a fence and get seats for the audience. Then it's ready!'

'How about practising a few circus acts as well?' said

Kalle sarcastically. 'Obviously you, Anders, only need to show yourself for people to get value for money, so you won't have to practise any clown numbers. But we've got to have some acrobatics and things as well!'

'I am going to ride,' said Eva-Lotta, eagerly. 'I'll borrow the bakery carthorse. Oh, it will be wonderful!'

She blew kisses at an imaginary audience.

'Equestrian acrobat Eva-Charlotta. Can't you just picture me?' she asked.

Kalle and Anders looked at her, their eyes full of worship. Oh yes, they could very easily picture her.

Fired with energy, the circus artists got to work. The place suggested by Eva-Lotta was definitely the best they could have found. The side wall of the bakery formed a suitable background for the performers. The grassy area in front was big enough for an arena and an audience. All it needed was a curtain that could screen the arena from the audience and be pulled open when the show started. A changing room for the artists presented a bigger problem, but Eva-Lotta's quick brain soon found a solution.

Above the bakery was a loft. Through a hatch on the side wall things could be hoisted up into the loft without the need of a staircase.

'And if things can go in, then things can also come out,' Eva-Lotta said. 'And the things that come out will be us. We can tie a rope up there and come swooshing down into the arena every time it's our turn to perform. When our act is over we can creep out without the audience noticing, scoot up the stairs and stay in the loft until our next number. It will be amazingly unusual, don't you think?'

'Yes, amazingly,' said Anders. 'And if you could get the bakery horse to swoosh down the rope it would be even more amazing. But that's going to be a bit harder. He's very tame and obedient, but there are limits, even for a horse.'

Eva-Lotta hadn't thought of that. But she wasn't going to give up her stunning idea.

'When it's my turn to ride then one of you will have to lead the horse through the audience. You make him stop under the hatch, and then boom—down I come, right onto his back.'

They got started on their preparations straight away. Kalle borrowed tarpaulins from his dad. Anders cycled to the timber yard on the outskirts of town and bought a sack of sawdust, which they spread over the arena. The rope was tied tightly to a beam in the loft and the three circus artists practised swooshing down until they almost forgot everything else.

In the middle of it all, Uncle Einar came sauntering up.

'Well, well, he's managed a whole afternoon on his own,' Eva-Lotta whispered to the boys.

'Which one of you wants to take this letter to the

postbox for me?' called Uncle Einar.

The three of them looked at each other. Actually, no one wanted to. But then Kalle's sense of duty took over. Uncle Einar was a mysterious person, and you had to keep an eye on the correspondence of mysterious people.

'I will!' he yelled.

Eva-Lotta and Anders looked at him in surprise.

'Just like a boy scout. Always prepared,' said Uncle Einar.

Kalle took the letter and ran off. As soon as he was out of sight, he looked at the address.

Miss Lola Hellberg. Stockholm Poste Restante it said.

'Post Restante' meant a person collected the letter themselves from the post office. Kalle knew that.

Weird, he thought. Why couldn't he have written her proper address?

He got his notepad out of his trouser pocket and opened it.

'List of suspected persons' it said at the top. Before, the list had contained a fair number of people. But with a heavy heart Kalle had been forced to cross them off one by one, because he had never succeeded in catching them in the act of committing a crime. So currently there was only one person on the list, and that was Uncle Einar. His name was underlined in red and underneath was a very detailed description of him. After the description was a new heading: 'Particularly suspicious circumstances'.

'In possession of a lock pick and a torch' it said. Kalle happened to have a torch himself, but that was a different thing entirely.

With a certain amount of difficulty he manged to fish a pencil stump out of his pocket, and resting against a fence he made the following observation in his notebook: 'Corresponds with Miss Lola Hellberg, Stockholm Poste Restante.'

Then he sprinted to the nearest postbox and a few minutes later was back at 'Circus Kallottan', as the circus project had been called after much discussion.

'What does that mean?' asked Uncle Einar.

'Kall for Kalle, Lott for Eva-Lotta and An for Anders, of course,' explained Eva-Lotta. 'And by the way, you mustn't watch while we're rehearsing.'

'That's a bitter blow,' said Uncle Einar. 'What am I supposed to do for the rest of the day?'

'Go and do some fishing by the river,' suggested Eva-Lotta.

'Stone the crows, do you want me to have a nervous breakdown?'

A *very* nervous disposition, thought Kalle.

Eva-Lotta, on the other hand, was merciless. Unrelentingly she drove Uncle Einar away, and the Circus Kallottan rehearsals continued with great energy. Anders was the strongest and most agile so it was only right for him to be the ring master.

'But I want to decide a tiny bit,' said Eva-Lotta.

'Fat chance,' said Anders. 'If I'm Ring Master, I decide.'

The ring master had made up his mind to have a top-notch acrobat troupe, and he made Eva-Lotta and Kalle practise for hours.

'There,' he said eventually, satisfied at last, as Eva-Lotta, smiling and erect in her blue leotard, stood with one foot on his shoulder and the other on Kalle's. The boys were standing with legs apart on the green see-saw, so Eva-Lotta was a little bit higher up than she was really comfortable with. But she would rather die than admit the butterflies she felt in her stomach when she looked down.

'It would be terrific if you could do a handstand while you're up there,' Anders managed to say, as he was trying to keep still without wobbling. 'That would go down well.'

'It would be terrific if you could sit on your own head for a while,' snapped Eva-Lotta. 'That would go down even better.'

Just then a most hideous sound echoed through the garden, an inhuman noise that came from a creature in deepest distress. Eva-Lotta cried out and took a death-defying leap down to the ground.

'What on earth is that?' she said. All three rushed away from the circus. The next second a furry grey bundle came hurtling towards them. It was the bundle that was making the atrocious noise. And the bundle was Tussy, Eva-Lotta's cat.

'Tussy! Oh, Tussy, what's the matter?' panted Eva-Lotta. She grabbed hold of the cat, not caring that it was scratching and biting.

'Oh, someone has . . . oh, that's wicked. Someone has tied this to her tail, to scare the life out of her.'

A piece of string was attached to the cat's tail and on the end of the string was a tin can, clattering loudly with every leap the cat made. Tears welled up in Eva-Lotta's eyes.

'If I knew who did this I would . . .'

She looked up. Two steps away from her stood Uncle Einar. He was laughing heartily.

'Ho, ho, that was the funniest thing I've seen in all my life.'

Eva-Lotta rushed up to him.

'Did you do this, Uncle Einar?'

'Do what? Strike a light, that cat can run! Why did you untie the can?'

Eva-Lotta screamed and beat him with her fists, while the tears streamed down her cheeks.

'It's horrible. Oh, it's cruel! I hate you, Uncle Einar!'

The cheerful neighing stopped. Uncle Einar's face underwent a strange transformation. It took on an expression of loathing that frightened Anders and Kalle as they stood as motionless spectators. He grabbed Eva-Lotta's arms hard and hissed:

'Calm down, girlie. Otherwise I'll crush every bone in

your body!'

Eva-Lotta took a deep, shuddering breath. Her arms were helpless in Uncle Einar's tight grip. She stared at him, terrified. Then he let go and ran his hand through his hair, rather embarrassed. He smiled and said:

'What *are* we doing? Having a boxing match, or what? I reckon you won that round, Eva-Lotta!'

Eva-Lotta didn't answer. She picked up the cat, turned on her heel and walked away, her head held high.

4

Kalle found it totally impossible to sleep when there were mosquitos in his room. Now another little perisher had woken him up again.

'Brutes,' he muttered. 'They shouldn't be allowed!'

He scratched his chin where the mosquito had bitten him. Then he looked at the clock. Nearly 1 a.m. A time respectable people ought to be sleeping!

'Talking of which,' he said to himself. 'I wonder if that cat-torturer is asleep.'

He padded to the window and looked out. There was a light on in the end window next door.

If he slept more then perhaps he wouldn't have such a nervous disposition, Kalle thought. And if he didn't have such a nervous disposition, maybe he would sleep more.

It was exactly as if Uncle Einar had heard him, because at that moment the light went out. Kalle was just about to go back to bed when suddenly something happened which made him open his eyes wide in surprise. After having a good look out of the open window and convincing himself that there was no one around, Uncle Einar climbed out onto the fire escape and after a second or two was on the ground. He was holding something under one arm. He walked swiftly towards the tool shed beside the bakery.

At first Kalle's brain stood still. He was so paralysed with astonishment that he couldn't think. But then a rush of thoughts, guesses and questions burst over him. He shook with suspense and excitement. Finally, finally, here was a genuinely mysterious person, not just at first glance but after closer observation. For this certainly was mysterious: an adult climbing out of a window in the middle of the night! He was up to no good otherwise he would have used the normal staircase.

'Conclusion number one,' said Kalle to himself. 'He doesn't want anyone in the house to hear him go out. Conclusion number two: he is up to some shady business—and oh, here I stand like a dunderhead, doing nothing!'

Kalle leapt into his trousers with a speed that would have impressed a fireman. He crept down the stairs as fast and as quietly as he possibly could, at the same time saying to himself: *please* don't let Mum hear me!

The tool shed! Why had Uncle Einar gone there? Crumbs, what if he had some tools in there he could use to kill people with! Kalle was perfectly ready to view Uncle Einar as the murderer he had long been searching for, a

Jekyll and Hyde figure who set off on an evil mission as soon as darkness settled over the town.

The tool shed door was partly open, but there was no sign of Uncle Einar. Kalle looked around him, uncertainly. There! Some distance away he spotted a shadowy figure hurrying away, but then the figure turned a street corner and was gone.

Kalle moved fast. He galloped off in the same direction. It was vital to hurry if he was going to prevent a horrendous crime! One thought struck him as he ran: what could he actually do? What would he say to Uncle Einar if he caught up with him? And what if he, Kalle, was the victim of Uncle Einar's crime? Perhaps he should go to the police? But you couldn't go to the police and say: 'This man has climbed out of a window in the middle of the night. Arrest him!' There was nothing in the law that prevented a man climbing in and out of windows all night long if he wanted to. It was probably not even against the law to have a lock pick. No, the police would only laugh at him.

And where was Uncle Einar, by the way? Kalle couldn't see him anywhere. It was as if the ground had swallowed him up! Oh well, in that case he didn't have to bother about him any longer. But it infuriated him intensely that he had lost the trail.

Even if he didn't want to get involved in open battle with Uncle Einar, it was naturally his duty as a detective to follow him and see what he was up to. A silent, unobtrusive witness who at some time in the future could step forward and say: 'Your Honour, on the night of the twentieth of June the man we see before us in the dock climbed out of a window on the top floor of master baker Lisander's house here in town, made his way down the fire escape, carried on to the aforementioned baker's tool shed situated in his garden and then proceeded to . . .' Yes, exactly. Where had he proceeded to? Kalle would never be able to answer that question. Uncle Einar had disappeared.

Kalle walked home, downhearted. At a street corner stood Constable Björk.

'What on earth are you doing out in the middle of the night?' he asked.

'Have you seen a man pass this way, Constable Björk?' Kalle interrupted him earnestly.

'A man? No, I haven't seen a soul other than you. Hurry on home to bed. That's what I would do, if only I could.'

Kalle went. No sight of a man. Well, everyone knew how much the police saw. A whole football team could pass by without them noticing! Although Kalle would make an exception for Constable Björk. He was better than other policemen. But 'Go home to bed' he had said! Would you believe it? The only person who really had eyes in his head was publicly ordered by the police to go home to bed! No wonder there were so many unresolved crimes. But it seemed there was nothing else to do than go home to bed. So that's what Kalle did.

The next day rehearsals for Circus Kallottan continued.

'Is Uncle Einar up yet?' Kalle asked Eva-Lotta.

'Search me,' answered Eva-Lotta. 'I hope he sleeps all morning so that Tussy doesn't get upset again.'

It wasn't long, however, before Uncle Einar appeared. He had a large bag of chocolates with him, and he threw it to Eva-Lotta.

'The circus prima-donna might need something to keep her going.'

Eva-Lotta struggled hard with herself. She loved chocolates, she really did, but her loyalty to Tussy demanded she throw back the bag with a feeble 'No thanks.' She weighed the bag in her hand, and found it hard to utter that feeble refusal. What about if she tasted one and threw back the rest? And then gave Tussy a herring? No, that was a pretty poor suggestion.

By now she had waited so long that the opportunity to make a grand gesture had passed.

Uncle Einar was walking on his hands, and returning a bag of chocolates to someone in that position was not easy. Eva-Lotta hung on to the bag, very well aware that it was meant as a gesture to patch things up. She decided to give Tussy two herrings and to treat Uncle Einar politely but coldly in future.

'Don't you think I'm clever?' asked Uncle Einar, once he was back on his feet again. 'Can't you take me on in Circus Kallottan?'

'No, adults aren't allowed to join in,' said Anders, in his role as Ring Master.

'Nowhere is there any understanding,' sighed Uncle Einar. 'What do you say, Kalle? Haven't I been treated harshly?'

But Kalle hadn't heard what he said. He was staring in fascination at an object that had fallen out of Uncle Einar's pocket while he was upside down. The lock pick! There it was in the grass. Kalle could easily take it. He gathered his thoughts.

'Harshly treated, did you say?' he replied, putting his foot over the lock pick.

'I'm not allowed to join in,' complained Uncle Einar.

'Shame,' said Eva-Lotta.

Kalle was pleased the attention had been moved from him. He could feel the lock pick under his bare foot. He ought to pick it up and say to Uncle Einar:

'You dropped this, Uncle!'

But he couldn't bring himself to do it. Instead he pushed it unobtrusively into his own pocket.

'To your places!' shouted the ring master, and Kalle

leapt up on to the see-saw.

It's a hard life, that of a circus artist. Practise, nothing but practise! The June sun beat down and the sweat streamed off 'The Three Desperados', Scandinavia's leading acrobatic troupe. That was what Eva-Lotta had called them on the neatly-printed posters they had put up around town.

'Would the desperate three like some buns?'

The Baker's jovial face appeared in the bakery window. He was holding out an oven tray full of newly-baked cinnamon buns.

'Thank you,' said the ring master. 'Afterwards, perhaps. You work better on an empty stomach.'

'Bunkum,' said Eva-Lotta. The bag of chocolates was empty and it felt as if her stomach was too, after all the gymnastisising.

'Yes, I think we deserve a little break,' said Kalle, wiping the sweat from his forehead.

'There's no point in me being ring master if you're going to decide.' Anders sounded rattled. 'The Three Desperados, huh! It ought to say "The Bun Desperados" on the posters.'

'You've got to eat to survive,' said Eva-Lotta, and she ran off to the kitchen to fetch some juice. And later, when the baker hurled a bag of buns out of the window, the ring master sighed despondently but was secretly rather glad. He ate more than anyone. They hardly ever had buns at home, and when they did they had to be shared between so many. His dad used to say 'There'll be some changes made around here' but he didn't mean more food, he meant more beatings! And since Anders thought he had experienced enough of those already, he kept away from home as much as possible. He preferred the atmosphere at Kalle's and Eva-Lotta's.

'Your dad's so kind,' said Anders, and sank his teeth into another bun.

'There's no one like him,' agreed Eva-Lotta. 'He's funny, too. He is so terribly fussy, he drives Mum mad, she says. And the thing he hates most is coffee cups with no handles. He says Mum, me and Frida do nothing but smash cup handles. Yesterday he bought two dozen new cups and when he came home he got a hammer and knocked off all the handles. "To save you the trouble," he said. Mum laughed so much she got a stomach ache,' went on Eva-Lotta, taking another bun. 'But Dad doesn't like Uncle Einar.'

'Then perhaps he'll knock off Uncle Einar's ears while he's at it,' said Anders.

'Who knows?' said Eva-Lotta. 'Dad likes family right enough, but having all Mum's aunties and uncles and second cousins twice removed loitering around the house makes him wish he was in solitary confinement in a prison cell far, far away.'

'I think that's where Uncle Einar ought to be,' Kalle blurted out.

'Hah!' said Anders. 'So the great detective thinks he knows something's going on, does he?'

Anders and Eva-Lotta laughed.

Yes, what do I know, really? thought Kalle a short while later, when rehearsals had finished for the day. I know nothing at all, that's what I know!

He felt downcast. But then suddenly he remembered the lock pick. He felt a jolt of excitement and expectation. He had a lock pick in his pocket and in some way he must try to use it. A locked door was all he needed. And why not try the same door Uncle Einar had opened? The door to the cellar in the castle ruins! Kalle didn't waste any more time thinking. He rocketed through the streets, hoping he wouldn't bump into someone he knew who would want to go with him. When he reached the top of the hill he ran along the winding path at such a speed that when he arrived at the locked door he had to rest for a few minutes to get his breath back. His hands were trembling as he pushed the lock pick into the lock. Would it work?

It didn't look like it at first. But he kept trying and suddenly he felt the lock give way. So that's how easy it was! He, Kalle Blomkvist, had opened a door using a lock pick! The hinges creaked as the door swung open. Kalle hesitated a moment. It felt pretty creepy going down into the murky cellar alone. He may only have come here to test the lock pick, but now he had access he'd be an idiot not to make the most of it and go down into the cellar again.

As he walked down the steps he felt a huge satisfaction knowing that he was the only boy in the entire town who had the opportunity to do this. And he was jolly well going to write his name on the wall a second time! If he and Anders and Eva-Lotta should ever in their lifetime come down here again, he would be able to show them his name on the wall in two places. Which meant he had been there twice.

Then he saw it. There were no names on the wall. They had been crossed out with a thick pencil so it was impossible to read what was written there.

'Aha, the plot thickens!' said Kalle out loud. Was it a ghost from the past who didn't like graffiti on the walls, and wiped out every trace? Kalle shuddered. But could you visualize a ghost equipped with a pencil? Kalle had to tell himself it was highly unlikely. But someone had done it!

'To think I didn't work it out straight away,' whispered

Kalle. 'Uncle Einar!' Naturally! Uncle Einar had tried to do all he could to stop them writing their names, and it was Uncle Einar who had crossed them out. He didn't want anyone who might possibly come down into the cellar to know they had been there. Kalle understood that much. But when had Uncle Einar done it? The names had definitely been there, untouched, when they left the ruins last time.

'Oh, what a knucklehead I am,' said Kalle. 'Last night, of course!'

Uncle Einar had been to the castle ruins in the night. That was why he had bought the torch. But had he really gone to all that trouble simply to rub out a few names on a wall? Kalle didn't think so. And what business did he have going into the tool shed? To get a pencil? Kalle laughed scornfully. Then he looked around to see if he could discover any clues left by Uncle Einar after his visit. A pallid light was falling through the openings high up in the wall, but it wasn't enough to light up all the corners and crevices. And anyway, it wasn't certain that Uncle Einar had stayed in that area closest to the staircase where the children had written their names. Dark passages branched out in all directions. Kalle had no desire to extend his tour of discovery into the gloomy vaults. And there would be no point, since he didn't have anything with him to light his way.

But one thing was certain: Uncle Einar would never

get his lock pick back. Kalle made up his mind about that straight away. He felt some opposition from his conscience, which told him you weren't allowed to keep something that didn't belong to you, but Kalle quickly silenced those thoughts. Why would Uncle Einar even have a lock pick? Who knew what doors he was planning to open with it! And if Kalle's opinion of Uncle Einar was correct, and he really was a shifty character, then essentially he was doing a good deed by taking the lock pick. Not only that—the temptation to keep it was far too great. Anders and Eva-Lotta and he could have their headquarters down here in the cellar. They would be able to investigate everything and maybe even discover what Uncle Einar wanted to do down here.

'That decides it,' said Kalle resolutely.

He was getting ready to leave when at the foot of the stairs he saw a small white object. Quickly he bent down and picked it up. It was a pearl. A gleaming white pearl.

5

Kalle lay on his back under the pear tree. He wanted to think, and he did that best in this positon.

'Naturally, it's possible the pearl has been there ever since the time of King Gustav Vasa five hundred years ago, when a careless noblewoman went down to the cellar for some beer and while she was she there lost her pearl necklace,' said Master Detective Blomkvist. 'But is that likely? When you are resolving the riddle of a crime,' he went on, turning on his side to look his imaginary listener in the eyes, 'You must always calculate the probability. And'—the Master Detective thumped his fist hard on the ground—'it is not probable that the pearl has been lying there for the past five hundred years, because surely there have been more boys like me with eyes in their head who would have found it. And by the way, if the pearl had been there as recently as the day before yesterday, when we were there, then a wide awake young man would have found it. Especially since I examined the ground pretty thoroughly. Yes, yes,' he waved a dismissive hand at his listener, who was clearly expressing admiration, 'Purely routine, that's all! What conclusions can we draw from this? In all probability that the so-called Uncle Einar dropped the pearl during his night-time visit to the castle ruins. Aren't I right?'

The imaginary listener obviously did not disagree, because Master Detective Blomkvist went on:

'Now we can ask ourselves: has Uncle Einar been seen dripping with pearls? Does he walk around sparkling with jewels?'

Kalle thumped his hand on the ground decisively.

'Certainly not! Therefore'—he grabbed his listener by the collar—'if this Uncle Einar is walking around strewing pearls to right and left then I am correct in seeing this as an extremely suspicious circumstance, am I not?'

No protests could be heard.

'Although,' continued the master detective, 'I am not a person to judge someone on evidence alone. The case must be resolved, and I believe I can say I am the right man for the job.'

Here his imaginary listener broke into such an outpouring of flattering remarks concerning Detective Blomkvist's ability to solve whatever it was, that even Detective Blomkvist himself thought he had gone too far.

'Now, now, no exaggerating,' he said kindly. 'The best detective who ever lived, that's a little over the top. Lord Peter Wimsey wasn't exactly stupid.'

He picked up his notepad. Under the heading 'Especially suspicious circumstances' he added: 'Makes night-time visits to castle ruins. Drops pearls.'

He read through everything he had written about Uncle Einar and was very satisfied. Now there was only one thing left in life that he wanted: Uncle Einar's fingerprints! He had been trying to get them all morning, fussing around his victim for hours, and leaving the ink pad, which belonged to his printing kit, in the sneakiest of places in the hope that Uncle Einar would by mistake put his thumb first on the ink pad and then on a piece of paper that just happened to be lying there. But oddly enough Uncle Einar had not fallen into the trap.

Well, thought Kalle, the only answer was to chloroform him out and take his fingerprints while he was unconscious.

'So this is where you're hiding, you dope. The performance is due to start in fifteen minutes!'

Anders hung over the fence, looking annoyed at the very relaxed Kalle. Kalle shot up. It wasn't easy being a detective *and* a circus performer. He crawled through the gap in the fence and caught up with Anders as he strode off.

'Has anyone come yet?' he puffed.

'I should say so,' answered Anders. 'Every seat is taken.'

'That means we're rich.'

'Eighteen kronor fifty,' said Anders. 'But you should have taken Eva-Lotta's place selling tickets instead of lying around in the grass leaving us to do all the work.'

They tore up the bakery staircase to the loft. There stood Eva-Lotta, looking through the crack between the hatch shutters.

'Full house,' she said.

Kalle went over and also had a look. There sat all the local kids and a whole load of out-of-towners as well. In addition, very prominently in the front row, was Uncle Einar. By his side sat the master baker and Mrs Lisander, and on the bench behind them Kalle spotted his own mum and dad.

'I'm so nervous my legs are about to collapse under me,' wailed Eva-Lotta. 'Be prepared for me to come plopping down on your heads during the acrobat number. And the horse is in such a bad mood I'm dreading the equestrian act.'

'Just don't embarrass us, that's all I'm saying,' said Anders.

'Play can commence!' called out Uncle Einar impatiently.

'We're the ones who decide that, I think,' snapped the ring master. But he put on his top hat anyway, or rather, baker Lisander's high white hat, opened the hatch, grabbed the rope and swung down into the arena. Eva-Lotta gave a blast on the trumpet and the audience applauded appreciatively. While this was going on, Kalle crept down the stairs to fetch the horse, which was tied to a tree. To the surprise and delight of the audience he led the horse between the seats. The ring master removed his hat, bowed politely and picked up a whip that was propped against the bakery wall. He cracked it in the air, loudly. Both he and the audience expected the bakery horse to set off at a trot around the arena, but the horse was not in that frame of mind. He merely stared stupidly at the audience. The ring master cracked the whip again and whispered loudly enough for the people to hear:

'Come on, dozy!'

Then the horse lowered his head and began to chew on a few blades of grass that were poking up through the sawdust. From the bakery loft came a giggle. The equestrian acrobat, waiting to make her entrance, couldn't stop herself laughing. Even the audience thought it was funny, especially Uncle Einar and Eva-Lotta's mum. At that moment Kalle decided to intervene. He took the horse's harness and led him to his position under the hatch. Eva-Lotta gripped the rope and prepared herself for a dramatic leap onto the horse's back. But suddenly the horse reacted. He made a hop worthy of a real circus horse and when Eva-Lotta came swishing down the rope, suddenly there was no horse to land on. She remained hanging from the rope, her legs kicking wildly, until Anders and Kalle managed to get the horse into reverse. Then Eva-Lotta glided down onto his back. Anders cracked the whip and the horse plodded very serenely around the arena. Eva-Lotta dug her bare heels into his side to get him to move faster, but without success.

'Traitor,' hissed Eva-Lotta.

But he was not going to be persuaded by any verbal encouragement. The plan had been for him to gallop round the arena at top speed so that his lively cantering would distract the audience's attention and they wouldn't notice that Eva-Lotta's tricks were fairly simple ones. But now that the baker's horse refused to become whole-heartedly involved it was clear the whole act was a little lame.

And to think of all the years I've been giving him oats, thought Eva-Lotta, bitterly.

Eventually the furious ring master cracked the whip right under the horse's nose, and it reared up onto its back legs in fright. This brought the act to a highly dramatic end and considerably increased the overall impression.

'But if the acrobat number also fails, we'll have to give them their money back,' said Anders in the loft afterwards. 'A circus horse, chewing grass. That's shameful! Now all we need is for Eva-Lotta to chomp on buns during the acrobat act!'

But Eva-Lotta didn't do that, and 'The Three

Desperados' were a dazzling success. Uncle Einar broke off a twig of white lilac and handed it to Eva-Lotta with a deep bow. The remainder of the programme wasn't quite up to the same high standard, but the clown act went down well, as did Eva-Lotta's song. In actual fact songs are not usually included in circus performances, but it was necessary to fill out the programme, and Eva-Lotta had written it herself. It was mainly about Uncle Einar.

'Oh, Eva-Lotta,' said her mother, when she had finished. 'You mustn't be so sarcastic about older people.'

'Yes, you must,' answered Eva-Lotta. 'When that person happens to be Uncle Einar.'

When the performance was over Mrs Lisander invited everyone for coffee among the lilac bushes in the garden. Grocer Blomkvist and master baker Lisander often sat among the lilacs in the evenings, talking politics. They told stories sometimes, too, and then Eva-Lotta, Kalle and Anders would sit with them and listen.

'Well, well, I do believe all the cups have handles today,' said the baker. 'The end of the world must have come. How are you, little Mia?' he said, with a kindly glance at his wife. 'Have you had so much to do today that you haven't had time to break any coffee cups?'

Mrs Lisander laughed heartily and offered Mrs Blomkvist a slice of sponge cake. The baker lowered his ample body into a garden chair and threw a sidelong look at his wife's cousin.

'Doesn't it get boring, walking around with nothing to do?' he asked.

'I'm not complaining,' answered Uncle Einar. 'I can get along without work. I only wish I could sleep better.'

'You can have one of my sleeping pills,' said Mrs Lisander. 'The doctor gave them to me when I had a pain in my arm, and I've got some left.'

'I'm thinking work would be better than sleeping pills,' said the baker. 'Get up tomorrow at four a.m. and help me bake the loaves, and I guarantee you'll sleep the next night.'

'Thanks, I prefer the sleeping pill,' said Uncle Einar.

Master Detective Blomkvist, who was sitting beside his mother on the opposite side of the table, thought to himself:

'One good way to sleep is to lie still in your bed. If you prowl around all night it's not surprising you don't get a wink of sleep. But if he takes a sleeping pill he'll soon drop off.'

Anders and Eva-Lotta had finished their drinks. They were sitting on the lawn, blowing blades of grass, very satisfied with the awful racket they were making. Kalle intended to join them. He knew the noise he could produce with the help of a blade of grass would beat most others. But at that very moment the idea struck him! The brilliant, genius idea, worthy of a master detective.

He nodded happily.

'Yes, that's the way to proceed!'

He rushed over, tore off a blade of grass, and blew a shrill and triumphant fanfare.

Naturally it wasn't risk-free, but a master detective had to take risks. If he wasn't prepared to do it then he might as well knock this detective business on the head and start selling hot dogs instead. Kalle was not afraid, but it was thrilling, scarily thrilling. He had set his alarm clock for 2 a.m. That seemed a suitable time. How long could it be before a sleeping pill started to work? Kalle wasn't entirely sure. But he thought Uncle Einar ought to be sleeping like a log at around two in the morning. Kalle couldn't believe otherwise. And that's when it would happen, because if you have finally found a Mysterious Person then you've got to get that person's fingerprints. Their description and birth marks and such things are important, obviously, but nothing can compare with a good, honest fingerprint.

Kalle took a final look through the window before slipping down under the covers. The white curtains in the window opposite billowed gently in the night breeze. There inside was Uncle Einar. Perhaps he was taking his sleeping pill at this very moment, before going to bed. Kalle rubbed his hands together in excitement. It wouldn't be at all difficult. Many, many times he and Eva-Lotta and Anders had used that fire escape, most recently in spring when they'd had a midnight feast in Eva-Lotta's loft. And if Uncle Einar could climb out, then Kalle could climb in.

'I'll do it at two, and that's for definite!'

Kalle crept into bed and fell fast asleep. He slept anxiously and dreamt that Uncle Einar was chasing him round the baker's garden. Kalle ran for his life, but Uncle Einar was catching up. Finally he grabbed Kalle's neck hard and said:

'Don't you know that all detectives must have a tin can tied to their tail, so people hear when they're coming?'

'But I haven't got a tail,' Kalle protested unhappily.

'Rubbish, of course you have. What do you call this?'

And when Kalle looked he did indeed have a tail, just like Tussy's.

'There you are,' said Uncle Einar, tying a tin can tightly to the tail. Kalle took a few leaps and the can made a horrible clattering sound. He was so miserable he could have cried. What would Anders and Eva-Lotta say, when he came rattling along like that? Never again would he be allowed to play with them. Nobody wants to be with someone who makes such a din. And there stood Anders and Eva-Lotta! They were laughing at him.

'That's what happens to detectives,' said Anders.

'Is it really true that all detectives have to wear a can on their tail?' pleaded Kalle.

'Absolutely,' said Anders. 'It's the law.'

Eva-Lotta put her hands over her ears.

'Help, what a noise!' she said.

Kalle had to admit that the noise was worse than ever. It clattered and rattled—oh, how it rattled . . . Kalle woke up. The alarm clock! Oh boy, what a racket! Kalle turned it off, and in an instant he was wide awake. Thank goodness, he didn't have a tail! There was much to be thankful for in this world. But now he had no time to waste.

He dashed to his desk drawer where he kept the ink pad. He shoved it into his pocket. Paper—he mustn't forget that. Then he was ready.

He padded down the stairs, more carefully than ever, avoiding the steps which he knew would creak. Mustn't give the game away!

Kalle felt quite exhilarated. He squeezed his body through the gap in the fence, and there he stood in the baker's garden. How still everything was. And how lovely the lilacs smelled! And the apple tree! Everything was completely different compared to the daytime. Every window was dark. Even Uncle Einar's!

A shudder went through Kalle as he put his foot on the fire escape. For the first time he felt an inkling of fear.

Was a fingerprint worth so much trouble? And he didn't really know what he wanted it for. But, he reasoned, Uncle Einar is probably a crook, and all crooks have their fingerprints taken. So, take Uncle Einar's fingerprint! 'Purely routine,' said the master detective encouragingly to himself, and began his climb up the fire escape.

'But if Uncle Einar is sitting up in bed wide awake, gawping at me as I poke my head in, what do I say then?'

Kalle's steps became more hesitant.

'Good evening, Uncle Einar. Beautiful weather tonight! I'm just having a little walk up and down the fire escape.' No, that wouldn't do!

I hope it was a *very* strong sleeping tablet Aunt Mia gave him, thought Kalle, trying to be brave. But despite that it still felt like sticking his head into a snake pit as he climbed onto the window ledge. It was dim in the room, but not so much that he couldn't see where he was going. At that moment Kalle resembled a curious little weasel ready to run at the first sign of danger.

There was the bed, and the sound of deep breathing was coming from its direction. Thank goodness, Uncle Einar was asleep! Kalle lowered himself extremely quietly from the window ledge. From time to time he stopped to listen, but nothing moved.

'Perhaps it was rat poison she gave him, seeing as he's sleeping so soundly,' thought Kalle. He lay on his stomach and wriggled cautiously towards his victim.

Purely routine!

What luck! Uncle Einar's hand was dangling over the side of the bed. All he had to do was take it and ... at that moment Uncle Einar mumbled something in his sleep and flung his hand over his face.

Thud, thud, thud. Kalle wondered if there was a steam engine hidden in the room, but it was only his own heart, hammering as if it wanted to come out.

Uncle Einar carried on sleeping, however. His hand was resting on the cover now. Kalle opened the lid of the inkpad and carefully, as if he were about to pick up a piece of burning coal, he took Uncle Einar's thumb and pressed it against the ink pad.

'Ahhh-puh,' said Uncle Einar.

Now all Kalle had to do was get the piece of paper. Where on earth was it? This was just perfect—here was his very own crook with ink on his thumb, everything was in place, and he couldn't find the paper! Wait, he had it! It had been there all the time, in his pocket. With enormous care he pressed Uncle Einar's thumb onto the paper. It was done! He had the fingerprint and he could not have been more content if he had been given a white mouse, which is otherwise what his heart desired more than anything.

Slowly crawl back and then swing your legs over the windowsill—it was so easy!

Well, everything would have gone according to plan

if Aunt Mia hadn't been so fond of pot plants. At the other end of the window sill, by the window that wasn't open, stood a dear little geranium in a pot. Kalle stood up slowly and . . .

For a second he thought it was an earthquake or some other natural catastrophe that had caused the tremendous crash. But it turned out to be a measly little flower pot.

Kalle stood up straight by the window with his back to Uncle Einar's bed.

I'll die now, he thought, and that's probably just as well.

With every fibre of his being he heard and felt and realized that Uncle Einar had woken up. Not surprising, really, when that flowerpot had made as much commotion as if it had been a whole florist's shop!

'Put your hands up!'

It was Uncle Einar's voice all right, yet not his. It sounded—yes, it sounded like cold steel.

It's always best to look danger straight in the eye. Kalle turned around, and looked right into the barrel of a gun. Oh, in his imagination he had done this many, many times and it had never bothered him in the slightest. With a quick move he had always caught off guard the criminal who was aiming at him, and with a 'Not so fast, my good man,' wrenched the pistol out of his hand. It was a little different in real life. Kalle had certainly been scared many times in his life: he had been scared when the bank manager's dog had flown at him in the town square once, and when he had fallen through the ice last winter, but never, ever, had he felt such paralysing, suffocating fear as he was feeling at this moment.

Mum, he thought.

'Come closer,' said the voice of steel.

How can you walk when you have soggy macaroni for legs? But he made an attempt.

'What on earth . . . is it you, Kalle?'

The steel had vanished from Uncle Einar's voice. But his voice was severe as he continued:

'What exactly are you doing in here in the middle of the night? Answer!'

Help me, wailed Kalle to himself. How am I going to explain?

At moments of extreme distress people sometimes get a flash of inspiration that will save them. Kalle recalled a few years ago, when he had taken to walking in his sleep. He had wandered about here and there during the night until his mum had taken him to the doctor's and he was prescribed tranquillizers.

'Well, Kalle,' said Uncle Einar.

'*How* did I get here?' asked Kalle. 'How did I get here? Don't tell me I've started sleep walking again? Oh, *now* I remember. I was dreaming about Uncle Einar (and that's the truth, thought Kalle), and I'm so sorry I bothered you!'

Uncle Einar put down the pistol. He patted Kalle's shoulder.

'Well, well, my dear master detective,' he said. 'I reckon it's all your detective ideas making you roam around in your sleep. Ask your mother to give you something to knock you out and it'll soon get better, you'll see. Now, I think I'd better see you out.'

Uncle Einar followed him down the stairs and opened the front door. Kalle loped across the grass with the speed of a greasy rabbit.

'Let me get home safely,' he whispered over and over again. He felt like a person who had just been rescued from a terrible shipwreck. His legs shook so oddly beneath him. He just about managed to drag himself up the stairs, and when he reached his room he sank down on his bed, panting.

He sat there for a long time.

It's dangerous work, being a detective! Some people thought it was purely a routine job, but was it heck. Before you knew it, you were facing a pistol. What about that? Kalle's legs were beginning to feel normal again, and the paralysing fear had gone. He pushed his hand into his trouser pocket. There was the precious piece of paper. Kalle was no longer afraid.

He was happy. Very carefully he put the slip of paper in his desk drawer. The lock pick and the pearl were already there. A mother looking at her child could not have looked more tenderly than Kalle as he studied the drawer's contents. He shut it gently and pocketed the key. Then he took out his notebook and turned to the page about Uncle Einar. A small addition had to be made, yet again.

'Has a pistol,' wrote Kalle. 'Sleeps with it under his pillow.'

The Lisander family ate breakfast on the veranda at this time of year. They had just started on their porridge when Anders and Kalle crept up in order to attract Eva-Lotta's attention. Kalle had been wondering whether Uncle Einar would bring up the subject of his night visitor, but Uncle Einar was eating porridge as if nothing had happened.

'Oh, Einar, how silly of me!' Mrs Lisander said suddenly. 'I completely forgot to give you that sleeping pill last night!'

7

'The best part of anything is the planning,' Anders had observed, immediately after their circus premiere. The actual performance was exciting enough, and lots of fun as well, but it was all the days filled with rehearsals and intensive preparations leading up to it that you remembered. The ex-circus performers lounged about, not really knowing what to do with themselves. Kalle was the one least affected by the lack of any meaningful activity. His detective business gave a purpose to his days, and occasionally his nights too. His surveillance work, which before had taken a more general direction, now concentrated wholly on Uncle Einar. Anders and Eva-Lotta often said they wished Uncle Einar would clear off, but Kalle dreaded the day when his very own crook would pack his bags and leave Kalle with no Mysterious Person to spend his time thinking about. And it would be infuriating if Uncle Einar left before Kalle had worked out exactly what kind of criminal he was. And he *was* a criminal, Kalle didn't doubt that for a second. Admittedly, Kalle's previous criminals had eventually been revealed to be perfectly decent people, or at least couldn't be found guilty of any foul deed, but this time Kalle was certain.

'There are so many clues, nothing else can be possible,' he said, to convince himself when he felt an occasional twinge of doubt.

But Anders and Eva-Lotta were not the slightest bit interested in the fight against crime, and they sat around feeling bored. However, as luck would have it, the post master's son Sixten happened to shout 'flirt' at Anders one day as he was walking down the High Street with Eva-Lotta. And this was despite the fact that currently there was peace between Sixten's gang and Ander's gang. Sixten was probably bored as well, which is why he wanted to stir things up.

Anders stopped. So did Eva-Lotta.

'What did you say?' said Anders.

'Flirt.' Sixten spat out the word.

'Ah,' said Anders. 'I hoped I'd heard wrong. Shame to have to teach you a lesson when it's so hot.'

'If that's all that's stopping you, I can put an ice cube on your forehead afterwards,' said Sixten. 'If you're still alive!'

'I'll see you this evening on the Prairie,' said Anders. 'Go home and prepare your mother as gently as you can!'

Then they went their separate ways. Anders and Eva-

Lotta went home, immensely cheered-up, to warn Kalle. It was turning into a feud, which would most definitely brighten up the summer holidays.

Kalle was completely preoccupied with observing Uncle Einar through the fence as he restlessly paced up and down the garden. To be honest, Kalle didn't want to be disturbed, but he couldn't help feeling pleased when he heard the news that Sixten had instigated another gang war. The three of them went to sit in Eva-Lotta's garden to discuss the situation, but just then Uncle Einar made an appearance.

'No one's playing with me,' he moaned. 'And what exactly is going on here?'

'It's a battle,' said Eva-Lotta. 'Anders is going to fight Sixten.'

'And who is Sixten?'

'One of the strongest lads in town,' said Kalle. 'Anders is bound to get hurt.'

'I'm sure I will,' Anders agreed happily.

'Do you want me to come and help?' asked Uncle Einar.

Anders and Kalle and Eva-Lotta stared at him. Was he seriously suggesting that they get an adult involved in their fight? And spoil everything?

'Well, Anders, what do you think of my suggestion?' said Uncle Einar. 'Shall I come too?'

'We-e-ll,' said Anders, feeling uncomfortable at having

to answer such a stupid question.

'No, that wouldn't be fair play.'

'No, maybe not,' agreed Uncle Einar, looking offended. 'But it would certainly do the trick. But you're probably too young to understand that. It's the kind of thing you learn later in life.'

'I hope he never learns anything so stupid,' said Eva-Lotta.

Uncle Einar whirled round and walked off.

'I have a feeling he was angry,' said Eva-Lotta.

'Hmm, adults can be weird at times, but that one is weirder than most,' said Anders. 'He gets trickier and trickier for every day that passes.'

If only you knew, thought Kalle.

The Prairie was a large piece of open ground on the edge of town. It was covered in bushes and undergrowth and was the domain of the town's youngsters. Here they were gold prospectors in Alaska and quarrelsome musketeers who fought violent duels. Camp fires were lit in the Rocky Mountains, lions were shot in Africa's jungles, noble knights charged about on their noble steeds and shady Chicago gangsters randomly aimed their machine guns, all depending on what film was showing at the local cinema. During the summer the cinema was closed, of course, but even so they were never at a loose end. There was generally one dispute or another to be settled, and there was always room on the

Prairie for peaceful games as well.

It was in that direction that Anders, Kalle and Eva-Lotta headed, with a feeling of tense expectation. Sixten was already there with his gang, whose members were called Benka and Jonte.

'Here comes someone about to see the blood spurt from his heart!' yelled Sixten, waving his arms wildly in the air.

'Who are your seconds?' asked Anders, totally ignoring the terrifying threat. His question was more a question of form; he knew very well who the seconds were.

'Jonte and Benka!'

'Here are mine,' said Anders, pointing at Kalle and Eva-Lotta.

'Which weapons do you prefer?' asked Sixten, in accordance with the rules. Everyone was aware that fists were the only weapons available, but sticking to the rules always gave a good impression.

'Knuckle sandwiches,' answered Anders, as was expected.

And then it started. The four seconds stood at a respectable distance but got so involved following the battle that the sweat poured off them. All that could be seen of the combatants was a blur of arms and legs and the occasional mop of hair. Sixten was the stronger of the two, but Anders was as speedy and nimble as a squirrel. He managed at the very start to land a couple of real blows on his opponent, but that only drove Sixten to an even greater desire to fight. It was looking bad for Anders. Eva-Lotta bit her lip. Kalle shot her a hasty look. He would love to have thrown himself into the scuffle for her sake, but unfortunately this time it was Anders who'd had the privilege of being called a flirt.

'Come on Anders!' shouted Eva-Lotta, encouragingly.

By this time Anders was also very angry. He launched himself into a grapple with Sixten and forced him to retreat. According to the regulations this kind of duel shouldn't last more than ten minutes. Benka held his watch in his hand, and both of the adversaries, who knew how precious time was, did their utmost to steer the fight in their own favour. But then Benka shouted 'Stop!' and it took every ounce of self-control for Sixten and Anders to obey his order.

'It's a draw,' said Benka.

Sixten and Anders shook hands.

'The insult is forgiven,' said Anders. 'But I'm planning to insult *you* tomorrow, so we can continue.'

Sixten nodded in agreement.

'That means war between the White Roses and the Red Roses.'

Sixten and Anders had named their gangs after the admirable examples from English history.

'Yes,' said Anders solemnly, 'Now it is war between the White Rose and the Red, and it shall send a thousand souls to death and deadly night.'

He had taken that quote from the history books, and he thought it rang out particularly beautifully now, with battle done and dusk falling over the Prairie.

The White Roses—Anders, Kalle and Eva-Lotta—shook hands sombrely with the Red Roses—Sixten, Benka and Jonte—and they went their separate ways.

The odd thing was that although Sixten assumed he had good reason to shout 'Flirt' at Anders as he came walking down the road with Eva-Lotta, he accepted her as a full and worthy opponent and representative of the White Roses.

The three White Roses headed for home. White Rose Kalle in particular was in a hurry. He couldn't feel entirely at peace unless he was keeping an eye on Uncle Einar every second.

Anders's nose was bleeding. Sixten had said his heart would be spurting blood, but it wasn't quite that serious.

'You fought a good fight,' said Eva-Lotta, admiringly.

'Oh, I wouldn't say that,' said Anders modestly, and looked at his blood-stained shirt. There was likely to be trouble when he got home. It was best to get it over with as soon as possible.

'See you tomorrow,' he said, and sped off.

Kalle and Eva-Lotta walked on together, until Kalle suddenly remembered that his mother had asked him to bring an evening paper home with him. He said goodbye to Eva-Lotta and carried on alone to the newspaper kiosk.

'All the evening papers are sold out,' said the lady in the kiosk. 'Try asking in reception at the hotel.'

Oh well, there was nothing else for it. Outside the hotel Kalle ran into Constable Björk.

Kalle felt proud to think that Constable Björk was practically a colleague. Of course, Kalle was a private detective, and private detectives as everyone knows are a notch or two above normal police officers, who frequently showed themselves to be incredibly clumsy when it came to solving even the most elementary cases. But in spite of that Kalle felt there was a connection between him and Constable Björk. They both fought crime in society. Kalle would very much like to ask Constable Björk for advice about one thing or another. In point of fact there was no doubting that for his age Kalle was an extraordinarily distinguished criminologist, but he was only thirteen years old. Generally he managed to ignore that fact, and in the process of his detective work he always saw himself as a mature man with penetrating, razor-sharp eyes and a pipe hanging nonchalantly from the corner of his mouth. A man who was known as 'Mr Blomkvist' and was treated with utmost respect by the law-abiding citizens of the town, while on the other hand regarded by the criminal element with deepest terror. But at this particular moment he felt only thirteen years old and he had to admit that Constable Björk had a considerably larger degree of experience than he had himself.

'All right, Kalle?' said Constable Björk.

'All right, thanks,' said Kalle.

Constable Björk threw an inquisitive glance at a shiny black Volvo that was parked outside the hotel.

'Stockholm registration,' he said.

Kalle stood next to him with his hands behind his back. For a long time they stood there in silence, thoughtfully studying the occasional passer-by taking an evening stroll across the square.

'Constable Björk,' said Kalle, all of a sudden. 'What do you do if you think someone is a crook?'

'Give him a thick ear,' said Constable Björk, jokingly.

'I mean, if he's committed some sort of crime,' said Kalle.

'Arrest him, of course,' said the police officer.

'Yes, but what if you only *think* he is and can't prove it?' persisted Kalle.

'Shadow him. Don't let him out of your sight!' Constable Björk gave a broad grin. 'I see you are dabbling in my work.'

I'm not dabbling, Kalle thought indignantly. No one ever took him seriously.

'Cheerio, Kalle. I'm off to the police station. Take care of my work while I'm gone!'

And with that Constable Björk left.

Shadow him, he had said! You couldn't shadow a person when they were already spending all their time sitting in the shade in the garden! Uncle Einar actually did precisely nothing. He lounged or sat or roamed about in the baker's garden like a caged animal, expecting Kalle and Anders and Eva-Lotta to entertain him to help pass the time. That was it—to help pass the time. It didn't seem as if Uncle Einar was on holiday at all, it was more as if he was waiting.

But for what? I can't work that one out, thought Kalle, as he walked up the steps to the hotel. The receptionist was busy so Kalle had to wait. There were two men standing at the desk.

'Can you tell me if a Mr Brane is staying at the hotel?' asked one of them. 'Einar Brane?'

The receptionist shook his head.

'Are you absolutely sure?'

'Yes, I am.'

The two men spoke quietly to each other.

'And no one calling himself Einar Lindeberg either?' asked the man who was doing all the talking.

Kalle gave a start. Einar Lindeberg? That was Uncle Einar! It is always a pleasure to be helpful to others, and Kalle was just about to open his mouth to tell them that Einar Lindeberg was staying at the baker's house when at the last minute he gulped, and all that came out was a cough.

'Phew, you almost made a blunder there, Kalle,' he said to himself, reprovingly. 'Let's just wait and see how this develops.'

'No, we have no one by that name, either,' said the receptionist firmly.

'I see! Well, I don't suppose you happen to know if someone by the name of Brane or Lindeberg has been staying in the town recently? Somewhere other than the hotel, perhaps?'

The receptionist shook his head again.

'Right you are! Can we book a room, please?'

'Certainly. I'm sure number 34 will suit you perfectly, gentlemen,' said the receptionist politely. 'It will be ready in ten minutes. How long are you planning to stay?'

'That depends. A couple of days, I guess.'

The receptionist offered them the register so they could sign their names. And Kalle bought his evening paper. He felt a strange excitement.

'The plot thickens, it most definitely does,' he said, under his breath. It was totally unthinkable for him to leave now, before he had a clear picture of these men who had asked after Uncle Einar. He knew for sure that the receptionist would be slightly astonished if he, Kalle Blomkvist, sat down in the hotel lounge and started reading the paper, but there was no other way. Kalle threw himself down in one of the leather armchairs in the manner of a salesman on a business trip, hoping with all his heart that the receptionist wouldn't come over and show him out. Luckily he had to answer the phone and had no time to pay Kalle any attention.

Kalle made two holes in the paper with his finger, at the same time worrying about how he would be able to explain this act of vandalism to his mother later. Then he tried to work out who these two men could be. Detectives, perhaps? Detectives usually turned up in pairs, at least in films. How would it be if he went up to them and said: 'Good evening, colleagues'?

'That would be stupid, if not to say stark staring mad!' Kalle answered his own question. You must never rush things.

But what luck he had sometimes! Both men walked over and sat down in the armchairs opposite Kalle. He could sit there and gawp at them through the newspaper as much as he liked.

'A description,' said the master detective. Purely routine! Right, the first one ... no, I ask you, it should be a punishable offence to look like that! Kalle had never seen anything quite so unpleasant before, and he thought the Make Our Town Beautiful Association would be willing to pay good money for this gent to leave the district. It was difficult to say what it was exactly that made his face so unpleasant. Was it the dome of his forehead, the eyes that were too close together, the cauliflower nose, or the mouth with its odd, lopsided leer?

If that isn't a crook, then I'm the archangel Gabriel, thought Kalle.

As for the other man, there was nothing particularly remarkable about his appearance, not counting his deathly-pale face, that is. He was short and had fair hair. His eyes were a very light blue and they scanned the room edgily.

Kalle stared at the men so hard it was surprising his eyes didn't appear on stalks through the peep holes. His ears were on high alert as well. The two men were having a lively conversation, but unfortunately Kalle couldn't hear much of it. Then suddenly the pale-faced man said in a high-pitched voice:

'He's got to be here, end of discussion! I saw the letter to Lola myself. The post mark clearly said Lillköping.'

Lola's letter? Lola! Lola Hellberg, who else!

My little grey cells are starting to work, Kalle thought with satisfaction. He had posted the letter to Lola Hellberg himself, whoever the lady in question could be. And her name was written in his book.

Kalle tried desperately to catch more of the men's conversation, but without success. Immediately afterwards the receptionist came over to tell them the room was ready. Nasty and Pale Face stood up and walked away. Kalle planned to do the same, until he noticed the receptionist wasn't at his desk. At that moment there was no one other than himself in the hotel reception. Without stopping to think he threw open the register and looked. Nasty had signed first, he had seen that. Tore Krok, Stockholm—that had to be him! And what was Pale Face's proper name? Ivar Redig, Stockholm. Kalle took out his little notepad and carefully wrote down the names and descriptions of his new acquaintances. He flicked through to Uncle Einar's page and wrote: 'Probably also uses the name Brane.' Then he tucked the newspaper under his arm and left the hotel, whistling merrily.

That left one thing: the car. Stockholm cars were so rare in this town that it had to be theirs. If they had arrived on the seven o'clock train, they would have booked a room hours ago. He made a note of the number plate and other distinguishing features. Then he checked the tyres. They were quite worn apart from the rear near-side one. It was brand new. Kalle drew a sketch of the tyre tread.

'Purely routine,' he said, and put the notepad into his pocket.

8

The Wars of the Roses broke out the following day, as agreed. Sixten found a note in his letterbox, full of the vilest insults. 'The truth of the above can be verified by Anders Bengtsson, leader of the White Roses, whose shoelaces you are not worthy to untie,' it said underneath, and with much grinding of teeth Sixten flew out in search of Benka and Jonte. The White Roses were on high alert in the baker's garden, expecting an attack by the Red Roses any minute. Kalle was balanced up in the maple tree, from where he had a good view down the street and all the way to the house where the post master lived. He was in charge of surveillance, both his own and on behalf of the White Roses.

'I haven't really got time for a battle,' he had told Anders. 'I'm busy.'

'Oh no,' groaned Anders. 'Not another crime. Has Fredrik the Foot had his hands in the collection money again?'

'Oh, forget it,' said Kalle. He knew it was pointless

looking for any understanding and he stayed put in the tree, as he had been commanded. Blind obedience to the leader was one of the golden rules of the White Roses.

There was one great advantage for Kalle being on surveillance duty, however, and that was because he could not only keep a watch on the Red Roses, but also on Uncle Einar. For the time being, the person in question was sitting on the veranda, helping Aunt Mia to pick the stalks from the strawberries. In reality that meant he de-stalked about ten and then lit a cigarette, sat on the veranda rail dangling his legs, teased Eva-Lotta as she scorched past on her way to the White Roses' headquarters in the bakery loft, and generally looked extremely bored.

'Aren't you finding this tedious?' Kalle heard Aunt Mia ask. 'What about having a walk around town, or going on a bicycle ride, or a swim or something like that. And by the way, there's a dance at the hotel every evening—I'm surprised you don't go there!'

'Thank you for your thoughtfulness, Mia dear,' said Uncle Einar. 'But I'm having such a restful time here in the garden that I haven't the slightest need to look for anything else to do. I'm really getting my strength back, and my nerves are recovering. I feel so calm and harmonious since I came here.'

Calm and harmonious? I don't think so, said Kalle to himself. He's about as calm as a pig in a sausage factory. I expect it's because he's so tremendously calm and harmonious that he can't sleep at night and keeps a pistol under his pillow.

'How long have I actually been here?' asked Uncle Einar. 'I can't seem to keep track of the days.'

'It will be fourteen days this Saturday,' said Aunt Mia.

'Well, I'll be a monkey's uncle! No longer than that? It feels as if I've been here a month, at least. Oh well, in that case I'd better start thinking of moving on.'

'Not yet, not yet,' Kalle pleaded silently, up in the tree. 'First I've got to find out why you are skulking here like a fox in its lair.'

Kalle was so distracted by the conversation on the veranda that he completely forgot he was supposed to be looking out for the Red Roses. He was brought back to reality by a whispered conversation on the street outside. There stood Sixten, Benka and Jonte, trying to look through the fence. They hadn't noticed Kalle in the tree above them.

'Eva-Lotta's mum and some bloke are sitting on the veranda,' reported Sixten. 'So we can't go through the front gate. We can take a circular route over the bridge and catch them by surprise from the side where the river is. I bet you they're in their headquarters up in the bakery loft.'

The Reds disappeared again. Kalle flung himself out of the tree and pelted off to the bakery where Anders and Eva-Lotta were passing the time by sliding down the rope that was still hanging there from their circus days.

'The Reds are coming!' yelled Kalle. 'They'll be over the river any second!'

The river was no more than a few metres wide where it flowed through the baker's garden. Eva-Lotta kept a plank there that could be used as a drawbridge when required. It made a fairly unreliable drawbridge, but if you ran fast and confidently you wouldn't fall in the water quite so often. And even if that did happen, the accident was usually limited to a pair of wet trousers because the depth wasn't worth worrying about.

The Whites eagerly hurried to get the drawbridge in place and then quietly hid themselves behind the elms lining the river bank. They didn't have to wait long. With mounting joy they watched as the Reds appeared on the other side, on the lookout for their foes.

'Ha! The drawbridge is down,' shouted Sixten. 'To battle! Victory is ours!'

He raced out onto the plank with Benka right behind him. This was the moment Anders had been waiting for. Quick as lightning he ran out, and just before Sixten set his foot on dry land he tipped the plank slightly—it didn't need more than that.

'That's exactly what happened to Pharaoh when he tried to cross the Red Sea!' shouted Eva-Lotta encouragingly to the floundering Sixten.

Then the Whites ran as fast as their legs would carry them back to the bakery, while Sixten and Benka, shouting revenge, crawled out onto the river bank. Anders, Kalle and Eva-Lotta took advantage of those precious seconds by barricading themselves inside the bakery loft. They made sure the staircase door was properly locked and the rope hauled up. Then they stood beside the open loft hatch and waited for their enemies. War cries announced their approach.

'Aw, did you get very wet?' Kalle asked Sixten sarcastically, as soon as Sixten appeared.

'About as wet behind the ears as you are all the time,' said Sixten.

'Are you coming out of your own free will or shall we smoke you out?' shouted Jonte.

'Oh, I think you can probably climb up and get us,' said Eva-Lotta. 'Will it matter if we pour boiling oil on your heads?'

Throughout the years there had been many feuds between the Red and the White Roses, but in reality there was no bad feeling at all between the members of the two gangs. Quite the opposite: they were the best of friends, and for them their feuds were nothing more than a really good game. There were no set rules for the battles, but they had one goal, and that was to cause the opposition as much trouble as they possibly could. Practically all means were allowed, apart from involving parents and other outsiders, naturally. Overrunning their opponents' headquarters, spying and springing surprise attacks on their enemies, taking hostages, uttering terrifying threats and writing insulting letters, stealing their opponents' secret documents and writing masses of them themselves, so that there were always plenty for their enemies to steal, smuggling vital papers across enemy lines—all these were important elements of the Wars of the Roses.

Currently the Whites were feeling immensely proud of their superiority.

'Move aside, if you don't mind,' said Anders politely. 'I'm just about to spit.'

Grumbling, the Reds retreated behind the corner of the bakery and tried unsuccessfully to open the door to the staircase.

But his success had made the Whites' leader a little too sure of himself.

'Tell the Reds I'm taking five minutes out to answer a call of nature,' he said, and threw himself down the rope. He calculated that he should be able to reach the little outside toilet with the red heart on the door before the Reds had even noticed he had left the loft. His calculation was not wrong. He slipped inside the outhouse and bolted the door shut. But he hadn't given any thought to his return journey. Behind the bakery corner lurked Sixten, and his face took on an almost heavenly glow when he realized he had his enemy trapped. It took him approximately two seconds to race to the outhouse and fasten the outside catch, and his triumphant laugh was the most evil, threatening sound that Eva-Lotta and Kalle had heard for a long time.

'Our leader must be freed from his horrendous imprisonment,' said Eva-Lotta determinedly.

The Reds, dizzy with joy, leaped about in a wild war dance.

'The White Roses have found new headquarters,' grinned Sixten. 'And from now on they will smell more beautiful than ever.'

'Stay here and insult them,' Eva-Lotta told Kalle. 'And I'll see what I can do.'

There was another staircase from the bakery loft, and that led directly down into the bakery. This gave Eva-Lotta an opportunity to get outside without the enemy noticing. She zig-zagged through the bakery, picking up a couple of biscuits in passing, and disappeared through the door at the other end of the building. Then she took a circuitous route and after some complicated manoeuvres managed to climb on top of the fence behind the outhouse without being observed by the Reds. Armed with a long stick she crawled up onto the outhouse roof. Anders heard something going on above his head and it gave him a glimmer of hope in his pitiful situation. While this was going on, Kalle was fully occupied hurling insults at Sixten and his companions in an attempt to keep their attention fixed on the bakery loft. There was one stupendously exciting moment when Eva-Lotta reached down with the stick to release the catch. If the Reds looked round now, all would be lost. Kalle tensely watched every movement Eva-Lotta made, and it took huge self-control for him to carry on hurling insults.

'You corking great turnip heads!' he said, just as Eva-Lotta's attempt succeeded. Anders felt the door give way and he galloped a hundred metres to one of the old elm trees. Thanks to many years of training it took him no time at all to scramble up into the tree, and when the Reds, as bitter about his escape as bloodhounds kept on a leash, chased after him and stood under the tree, he yelled that he would batter the first person who climbed up the tree so badly even his own mother wouldn't recognize him. At the last minute Sixten remembered Eva-Lotta. She was just about to reach safety but it soon became apparent that she had bought her leader's freedom at the expense of her own. The Reds surrounded the outhouse and Eva-Lotta fell like a ripe fruit into their waiting hands as she was about to clamber down the fence.

'Quick, take her to our headquarters!' roared Sixten.

Eva-Lotta defended herself with the courage of a lioness, but it was Benka and Jonte's combined strength that forced her to submit. The Whites prepared to race to her rescue. Kalle slid down the rope and Anders took a reckless leap from the elm tree. But while Benka and Jonte pushed and dragged Eva-Lotta towards the river, Sixten kept the rescuers at bay with such fierce fighting that the Reds were easily able to reach the river with their prisoner of war. Getting a struggling Eva-Lotta over the drawbridge was clearly going to be impossible, so Benka shoved her into the water and then he and Jonte plunged in after her.

'No resistance, otherwise we'll have to drown you,' said Jonte.

The threat didn't stop Eva-Lotta from trying to fend them off worse than ever, and she was delighted when she managed to drag Benka and Jonte under the water a couple of times. True, she went under herself at the same time, but that didn't spoil her satisfaction.

On the slope down to the river, the battle continued with ferociously. The din was so overwhelming that Mr Lisander the baker found it necessary to leave his bread dough to see what was going on. He wandered leisurely down to the river, where his daughter's dripping head was just popping up after another ducking under the water. Benka and Jonte let go of Eva-Lotta and looked guiltily at the baker. Even the battle up on the river bank died down. The baker took a long look at his child and for a few moments said nothing.

'Well, Eva-Lotta, can you do the crawl?' he said eventually.

'Of course I can,' answered Eva-Lotta. 'I know all the different strokes.'

'Oh, right. I was just wondering,' said the baker, considerately, and wandered back to the bakery.

The Red Roses had their headquarters in the garage belonging to the post master's house. No car was kept there for the time being, which is why Sixten had taken it over for his own purposes. Here he kept his fishing rod and his football, his cycle and his bow and arrows, a goal-keeper's net, and all the Red Roses' secret documents. This is where Eva-Lotta was imprisoned, dripping wet, although Sixten very nobly said she could borrow his track suit.

'Chivalry towards the defeated, that's my motto,' he said.

'Tosh, I'm not defeated one bit,' said Eva-Lotta. 'I'll be set free soon. But while I'm waiting let's practise a few goals.'

The prison guards had no objection.

Anders and Kalle stayed by the river, having serious discussions. It was humiliating that they hadn't been able to capture Sixten and been able to organize an exchange of prisoners.

'I'll sneak over there and have a look around,' said Anders. 'You get back up the maple tree again and keep a lookout, in case they decide to come back here. Defend our headquarters to the last man! And if you are overpowered, burn all our secret papers!'

Kalle realized it would be quite hard to follow that order to the letter, but he didn't protest.

That maple made an excellent watchtower! You could sit in comfort where a branch joined the tree trunk, well-hidden by leaves and with a view over the baker's front garden and the whole street as well, right up to corner where it met the High Street. Kalle felt energized by the battle he had fought, but he also had a guilty conscience. He knew he had neglected his duty to society. If the Wars of the Roses hadn't intervened, he would have been standing guard outside the hotel from early morning, shadowing the two men who had arrived the previous evening. It might have taken him a step closer to solving the mystery.

Uncle Einar was pacing up and down the garden path below. He didn't see the spy in the tree, so Kalle was free to observe him. Every move he made was impatient or annoyed, and his face was such a picture of restlessness and boredom that Kalle almost felt sorry for him.

Perhaps we ought to let him join in our games after all, thought Kalle, feeling a rush of sympathy.

The street on the other side of the fence was deserted. Kalle peered in the direction of the Postmaster's house. It was from that direction he could expect an attack. But there were no Red Roses in sight. Kalle glanced in the other direction, up towards the High Street. Here were some people! It was—no, it couldn't be—yes, it was! It was those two characters, what were they called again? Krok and Redig, that was it! Immediately Kalle felt as tense as a coiled spring. They were coming closer and closer. Just as they passed the baker's gate they spotted Uncle Einar. And he spotted them.

It was horrible to see the way the colour drained from Uncle Einar's face in a flash, Kalle thought. He could not have been whiter if he had been a corpse. And a rat, suddenly realizing it is trapped, could not have looked so desperately afraid as Uncle Einar as he stood on the other side of the gate.

One of the two men began to speak. It was the short, washed-out one—Redig. His voice sounded incredibly soft and gentle.

'Well, well, look who we have here. Einar,' he said. 'Our dear old Einar!'

Kalle felt a shiver run down his spine. It was the voice that had caused it. It was so smooth on the surface, but it sounded as if there was something very nasty and dangerous underneath.

'You don't seem particularly pleased to see us, old friend,' purred the smooth voice.

Uncle Einar clung onto the gate with a pair of trembling hands.

'Ye-e-s,' he said. 'Of course I am. But you turned up so unexpectedly.'

'Did we?' Pale Face smiled. 'Well, you forgot to give us your forwarding address when you scarpered. Absent-minded, I expect. Luckily you wrote a letter to Lola with a more or less legible postmark on it. And Lola is a sensible girl. If you have a serious word with her, she isn't one to keep things to herself.'

Uncle Einar was breathing hard. He leaned over the gate towards Pale Face.

'What have you done to Lola, you . . . !'

'All right, all right,' the smooth voice interrupted him. 'Don't get yourself in a tizz. Peace and quiet, rest and relaxation, that's what you want on your holiday. Because this is a little holiday visit, I assume?'

'Yes—yes,' answered Uncle Einar. 'I came here to have a little rest.'

'I quite understand! You've been working so hard lately, haven't you?'

Pale Face was doing all the talking. The one Kalle had called Nasty merely stood there silent and smiling—but it wasn't what Kalle would call a friendly smile.

If I bumped into him on a dark street I would suddenly be afraid of the dark, he thought. Although the question was: wouldn't it be worse to bump into Pale Face, Ivar Redig?

'What exactly are you trying to say, Arthur?' asked Uncle Einar.

Arthur—his proper name is Ivar, I know that, thought Kalle. But crooks and swindlers always have so many different names.

'You know damned well what I'm trying to say,' said Pale Face, and his voice had hardened. 'Come with us for a little drive and we can discuss it.'

'I've got nothing to discuss,' said Uncle Einar, vehemently.

Pale Face took a step closer.

'Oh, haven't you?' he said softly.

What was that he was holding? Kalle had to lean forward to see.

'Oh, that's torn it,' whispered Kalle. Now it was Uncle Einar's turn to be staring down the barrel of a gun.

Strange habits some people had, walking around with guns in the middle of the week!

Pale Face stroked the shining metal before he went on:

'Have another think and I'm sure you'll come with us.'

'No!' shouted Uncle Einar. 'No! I haven't got any business with you. Go away, otherwise . . .'

'Otherwise you'll call the police, eh?'

Both the men outside the gate laughed.

'Oh no, Einar, I don't think that's likely! You're just as keen to keep the police out of this as we are.'

Pale Face laughed again, an odd, ugly laugh.

'Imagine you planning it so well, Einar! I have to admit the idea was a good one. A little holiday, incognito, until the worst of the hullaballoo has died down. Much cleverer than trying to flee abroad.'

He fell silent for a moment.

'But I reckon you've been just a bit too clever this time,' he continued. 'It never pays to try and fool your mates. Too many were forced to stop at a very early age when they tried that. It's just not on for three people do the job and only one get all the takings.'

Pale Face leaned over the gate and glared at Uncle Einar with such an expression of hatred that it made

Kalle start sweating up in the tree.

'Do you know what I'd really like to do?' he said. 'I'd like to blast a bullet right through your body as you're standing here, you scrawny, cowardly louse!'

This seemed to bring Uncle Einar to his senses.

'And what would that achieve?' he said. 'Are you so desperate to get locked up again? Shoot me and in five minutes the cops will be here. What do you gain by that? And surely you don't imagine I'm walking around with it on me? No, put that little toy away'—he pointed at the pistol—'and let's discuss this sensibly. If you can behave nicely I might be willing to share.'

'Your generosity knows no bounds,' said Pale Face sarcastically. 'So, you're willing to share? Pity you came up with such a brilliant idea too late. Much too late! Because you see, dear Einar, we don't want to share. You can have a while to mull it over—let's be generous and say five minutes—and then you can hand the whole kit and caboodle over to us. I hope for your own sake that you understand what we're saying.'

'And if I don't? I haven't got it here, and if you do me in there won't be anyone to help you find it.'

'Einar, old friend. You must believe I was born yesterday. There are ways to make people see reason, very good ways. I know what you're thinking now. I know it just as if I could look right into that rotten skull of yours. You think you can trick us a second time! You think you can stall us with your talk of sharing and then you'll quietly hop it, wiping every trace of your footprints from the face of the earth before we have time to stop you. But I'll tell you one thing! We will stop you, and in a way you'll never forget! We'll be staying in town for a while, Ivar and me, and you'll be seeing quite a lot of us. Every time you set foot outside this garden gate you'll bump into your dear old mates. And there will come a time when we will be able to talk undisturbed, believe me.'

He gave what was probably an ominous grin, as it says in books, thought Kalle, and studied Pale Face thoughtfully. As he leaned forwards to see better, there was the crack of a twig. Uncle Einar threw a swift glance around him to see where the sound had come from, and Kalle went ice cold with fear.

'Please don't let them see me! Please don't let them! Otherwise they'll liquidate me.'

He realized that if he was discovered his situation could be exceptionally dangerous. It wasn't likely that a man such as Pale Face would show much mercy to a witness who had happened to overhear the last three minutes' conversation. Luckily, none of the three men seemed interested in investigating the cause of the little interruption. Kalle breathed a sigh of relief. His heart had returned to its normal place when suddenly he saw a sight that made it rapidly leap up into his mouth again. Someone was coming along the street. A small figure in a red track suit that was far too big. It was Eva-Lotta. She was merrily swinging a sopping wet dress and singing the song she liked so much: '*A sailor went to sea, sea, sea, to see what he could see, see, see.*'

Please don't let her see me, whimpered Kalle to himself. Because if she says 'Hey there, Kalle,' it could be very dangerous indeed.

Eva-Lotta came closer.

'Of course she'll see me. Of course she'll want to look up at our surveillance tree. Oh no, why did I ever climb up here!'

'Hello, Uncle Einar,' said Eva-Lotta.

If Uncle Einar was usually very glad to see Eva-Lotta, on this occasion he looked practically delirious with joy.

'What a good job you turned up, little Eva-Lotta,' he said. 'I was just about to go in and see if your mum had dinner ready. Come on, let's go together!'

He waved at the two men outside the gate.

'Cheerio, lads,' he said. 'Unfortunately I have to leave you now.'

'Farewell, dear old Einar,' said Pale Face. 'We'll meet again, rest assured.'

Eva-Lotta looked questioningly at Uncle Einar.

'Aren't you going to ask your old friends to come in and have dinner with us?' she said.

'You know what, I don't think they've got time.'

Uncle Einar took hold of Eva-Lotta's hand.

'Another time, little miss,' said Nasty.

Now . . . now she'll do it, thought Kalle, as Eva-Lotta passed under the maple tree. Oh no!

'But all that he could see, see, see . . .'

Eva-Lotta sang and threw her usual glance up at the hideaway in the tree, the White Roses' lookout post. Kalle stared directly into her cheerful blue eyes.

For many years they had been involved in the Wars of the Roses. They had taken part in quite a few terrible feuds, and played spies and secret agents, and there were two things they had learned: never be surprised and keep your mouth shut when necessary. There is your accomplice, up in the maple tree, but he is holding a warning finger to his lips and his entire expression is pleading: 'Keep quiet!'

Eva-Lotta walked on with Uncle Einar.

' . . . *was the bottom of the deep blue sea, sea, sea.*'

10

'And what is Mr Blomkvist's opinion of that extraordinary conversation?'

Kalle was lying on his back under the pear tree in his own garden, being interviewed again by his imaginary listener.

'Well,' replied Mr Blomkvist, 'First and foremost, it is apparent that in this crime scenario we have not one but three crooks. And I warn you, young man (the imaginary listener was especially young and inexperienced), I warn you! Much will happen in the coming days. It would be wise if you stayed indoors after dark. Clearly this will be a battle of life and death, and anyone who is not used to mixing with the dregs of society can easily find their nerves in shreds.'

Mr Blomkvist himself was so accustomed to mixing with the dregs of society that his nerves could stand the strain. He removed the pipe from his mouth and continued:

'You see, these two gentlemen, Krok and Redig—and

I'm sure I don't need to tell you that those are not their real names—these two gents are going to make things very uncomfortable for Uncle Einar. I mean, Uncle Einar Lindeberg or Brane, as he also calls himself. To put it bluntly—his life is in danger!'

'And what side will Mr Blomkvist choose in this conflict?' asked the listener breathlessly.

'Law and order, young man, law and order! As always! Even if it demands my life.' The master detective smiled a sad smile. For the sake of law and order he had already faced a thousand deaths, so one more wouldn't make much difference.

His thoughts ran on.

But I would give anything to know what they want from Uncle Einar, he said to himself, because now he was Kalle again, a very uncertain Kalle, who thought everything was turning rather nasty.

Then all of a sudden he remembered the newspaper! That newspaper Uncle Einar had bought shortly after he arrived, when they were sitting in the café garden. It was safe and sound in the left-hand drawer of Kalle's desk, but Kalle hadn't bothered to take a closer look at it.

'An unforgiveable error,' he reproached himself, and shot up.

He recalled that Uncle Einar had been especially eager to read the *Latest News* page.

All he had to do now was work out what had interested

him so much. *New nuclear bomb test*—hardly. *Brutal attack on old man*—could that be it? No, it said here that two youngsters in their twenties had attacked an older man when he wouldn't give them any cigarettes. Uncle Einar couldn't have been involved in that. *Massive jewellery heist in Stockholm's wealthiest neighbourhood*—Kalle whistled, and read the article at lightning speed.

A huge robbery took place in the early hours of Saturday morning in an apartment in Östermalm. The apartment, owned by a well-known Stockholm banker, was unoccupied that night, which explains why the thieves were able to carry out the burglary undisturbed. It is assumed they gained entrance by forcing open a kitchen window. The jewellery, calculated to be worth 100,000 kronor, was held in a safe, which someone carried away from the property between the hours of 2 and 4 a.m. It was found on Saturday afternoon blown open and empty in a wood thirty kilometres north of the city. Detectives from the Criminal Investigation Unit's robbery division, who raised the alarm early on Saturday morning, have so far found no clues to go on. It is thought that at least two and possibly more people were involved in the heist, which is considered to be one

of the most daring robberies to have occurred in this country. Detectives have informed all police stations in the country, and security has been stepped up at all ports and borders since it is thought that the burglars will have to leave the country in order to get rid of the goods. The stolen goods include an extremely valuable platinum and diamond bracelet, a large quantity of diamond rings, a gold brooch encrusted with four diamonds, a choker of oriental pearls, and an antique gold and emerald pendant.

'You numbskull, you stonking great numbskull!' said Kalle to himself. 'How could you have missed that! Lord Peter Wimsey and Hercule Poirot would have worked it out ages ago. It was all there in the article!'

He held the pearl in the palm of his hand. How could you tell if a pearl was oriental?

A thought struck him like a blow on the head. 'I'm not walking around with it on me,' Uncle Einar had said. No, of course not! And he, Kalle Blomkvist, knew where it was, the bracelet and all the platinum and diamonds and emeralds and all the rest! In the castle ruins, naturally! Uncle Einar didn't dare have it with him in his room. He had to hide it somewhere safe. And the cellar of the castle ruins was a perfect place. No one ever went there.

Thoughts raced in Kalle's head. He must go to the ruins and try to find the valuables before Uncle Einar took them away. Oh, and he must also follow Uncle Einar and those other two, so that he could arrest them on the spot! How would he have time for all of that?

And in the middle of the Wars of the Roses, as well! No, he couldn't solve the crime without assistance. Not even Lord Peter Wimsey could pull that off. He had to tell Anders and Eva-Lotta, and ask for their help. Okay, they never did anything but mock his detective operations, but this time it was different.

A small voice inside Kalle told him that in this instance he should be seeking assistance from the police, and he knew the voice was right. But if he did go to the police and told them everything, would they believe him? Wouldn't they merely laugh at him, like adults usually did? Kalle had nothing but bad experience from his earlier attempts in the detective branch. Nobody wanted to believe you were capable of anything when you were only thirteen. No, he would wait until he had gathered more evidence.

Carefully, Kalle placed the pearl in the drawer. Look, there was Uncle Einar's fingerprint! Who knew when that would come in useful? He was very glad he'd thought to get it.

So far the police have no trace of the suspects the newspaper had said. Same old story! But they might have managed to get fingerprints at the scene of the crime! Fingerprints—if a burglar had past history with the police, then his fingerprints would be on the police register. Then all you had to do was compare them with the ones found at the scene and ta dah, problem solved! Then you could definitely say 'This break-in was committed by Fredrik the Foot!' Well, yes, if it was Fredrik the Foot's prints they had found, that is. But on the other hand the person who committed the burglary might not have his fingerprints on the register, so that wouldn't be much help.

But as luck would have it, Kalle *did* have Uncle Einar's fingerprint on a small scrap of paper. A very good, clean fingerprint. And very slowly an idea took shape in his head. He could give the police a helping hand, seeing as they 'had no clues to go on'. If it really was the break-in in Östermalm that Uncle Einar had been involved in—naturally Kalle couldn't be absolutely sure, but the evidence pointed in that direction—then perhaps the Stockholm police would be very interested in that scrap of paper with Uncle Einar's thumbprint.

Kalle took out a pen and a piece of paper. And he wrote:

To the Criminal Investigation Unit, Stockholm Police

Then he chewed the pen for a while. It was important

to write it so they would assume it had been written by an adult. Otherwise they would probably toss the letter in the wastepaper basket, the blockheads! Kalle continued:

Since it appears from the newspapers that a burglary has been comitted in the Östermalm area and because perhaps your good selfs have obtained some fingerprints I enclose ditto in the hope that it matches some you have. Further information can be provided with no charge and post free from

KARL BLOMKVIST
Private detective
14 High Street
Lillköping

He hesitated a little before he wrote 'private detective', but then he thought it was unlikely that the Stockholm police were ever going to see him, so they might as well live in the belief that the letter was written by a Mr Blomkvist, private detective, and not Kalle, 13 years old.

'That's that,' said Kalle, and he licked the envelope and sealed it.

And now, full speed to Anders and Eva-Lotta.

11

Anders and Eva-Lotta were in the bakery loft, the headquarters of the White Roses. It made an excellent hideaway. Apart from being their headquarters the old loft served as a bakery storehouse and a dumping ground for old furniture. There was a white chest of drawers, recently banished from Eva-Lotta's bedroom, a pile of ancient chairs crowded in one corner, and there was also a battered dining room table, long past its best, where they played ping-pong on rainy days. But Anders and Eva-Lotta didn't have time for ping-pong right now. They were concentrating on making 'secret documents'. As each one was finished Anders put it in the tin box, which was the White Roses' most precious possession. There they kept memorabilia from previous Wars of the Roses: peace treaties, secret maps, pebbles with strange markings, and a whole heap of other things that looked to outsiders like junk. But for the members of the White Roses the contents represented cherished treasures, for which they were prepared to shed their own blood. Their leader wore the key on a piece of string around his neck, day and night.

'I wonder where Kalle's got to,' said Anders, as he put a completed document in the tin box.

'He was sitting in the maple tree a minute ago,' said Eva-Lotta.

That very second Kalle came bursting in.

'Stop that!' he panted. 'We must make peace with the Red's immediately, even if it means unconditional surrender.'

'Are you demented?' said Anders. 'We've only just started.'

'Can't be helped! We have more important things to do. Eva-Lotta, do you like Uncle Einar a lot?'

'What do you mean, a lot?' asked Eva-Lotta. 'Why would I be especially fond of him?'

'Because he's your mum's cousin.'

'As far as that's concerned, I have a hunch Mum doesn't like him much herself, so I'm not crazy about him, either. But why are you asking?'

'Then you won't be upset if you hear that Uncle Einar is a crook?'

'What? Cut it out, Kalle,' said Anders. 'It was Fredrik the Foot who stole the collection money, not Uncle Einar!'

'Shut up! Read this before you say anything else,' said Kalle, and he showed them the newspaper.

Anders and Eva-Lotta read the article about the *Massive jewellery heist in Stockholm's wealthiest neighbourhood.*

'And listen to this,' said Kalle.

'How do you feel, *actually*?' asked Anders, sympathetically. He pointed a dirty finger at another article: *Mad cow causes panic*. 'Do you think that could have been Uncle Einar as well?'

'Shut up, I said! Eva-Lotta, you saw those blokes, the ones talking to Uncle Einar by the gate a minute ago? They were his partners in crime, and Uncle Einar has tricked them somehow. Krok and Redig, that's what they're called, and they're staying at the hotel. And the jewellery is hidden in the castle ruins.'

The words poured out of Kalle's mouth.

'In the castle ruins? But you said they were staying at the hotel,' said Anders.

'Krok and Redig are! But the jewellery, idiot—that's the emeralds and platinum and diamonds, don't you see? Crikey, when I think about it, there are jewels worth a million kronor down in that cellar!'

'How do you know that?' asked Anders, sounding extremely doubtful. 'Has Uncle Einar said so?'

'Some things you have to work out for yourself!' said Kalle. 'When you are solving the mystery of a crime you must always include probability.'

That was master detective Kalle Blomkvist making a

brief appearance, but he soon vanished and in his place was Kalle, eagerly gesticulating and worried that he wouldn't be able to convince the other two. It took him a good while. But he succeeded. After he had told them everything and reported his observations, his night-time visit to Uncle Einar's room, the discovery of the pearl in the castle ruins and the conversation he had overheard from up in the maple tree, even Anders was impressed.

'Mark my words, this lad will be a detective when he grows up,' he said, approvingly. Then his eyes began to glitter.

'Oh, what fun! What an opportunity! We haven't got time to waste on stuff like the Wars of the Roses.'

'That explains it,' said Eva-Lotta. 'Now I know why I can't keep my hands out of the biscuit tin. I'm as light-fingered as Uncle Einar. That's what happens when you are related to a criminal. Right, he has to get out of our house, and I mean now! What if he steals the family silver!'

'You don't have to worry about that at the moment,' said Kalle. 'He's got more important things to think about than the silver, believe me. He's in a terrible fix because Krok and Redig will be watching him like a hawk.'

'So that's why he went for a lie-down after lunch. He said he was feeling sick.'

'You *bet* he was feeling sick,' said Anders. 'Now, first of all we've got to make peace with the Reds. Eva-Lotta, you hoist the truce flag and go over there and explain everything. Naturally they'll think we've gone bonkers.'

Obediently Eva-Lotta tied a white handkerchief to a stick and trotted off to Sixten's garage, where her message of unconditional surrender was met with both astonishment and disappointment.

'Are you off your heads?' asked Sixten. 'We've only just got going.'

'We surrender unconditionally,' said Eva-Lotta. 'You've won. But we'll humiliate you again soon, and then just watch the sparks fly!'

Sixten reluctantly agreed to a peace treaty, but it included hard terms for the Whites, such as when they received their pocket money they had to put half aside to buy sweets for the Reds, and when the Whites passed the Reds on the street they were to bow three times and say 'I know I am not worthy to tread the same ground as you, oh master.'

Eva-Lotta signed the treaty on behalf of the White Roses, formally shook hands with the Reds' leader, and pelted back to bakery loft. As she went through the front gate she couldn't help noticing one of Uncle Einar's 'friends' waiting on the pavement opposite.

'Official guard duty has started,' she reported to Anders and Kalle.

'This will be a much better war than the Wars of the Roses, I'm sure,' said Anders gleefully. Kalle, what do you reckon we should do now?'

Even if under normal circumstances Anders was the leader, he realized that in this specialized area he should hand the position of authority to Kalle.

'First and foremost, look for the jewellery! We've got to go to the castle ruins. But someone has to be at home and keep an eye on Uncle Einar and the other two.'

Kalle and Anders looked hopefully at Eva-Lotta.

'Not on your life,' said Eva-Lotta, determinedly. 'I want to look for the jewellery too. And anyhow, Uncle Einar is in his bed pretending to be ill, so I don't suppose anything will happen while we're gone.'

'We can put a matchbox outside his door,' suggested Kalle. 'And if it's still in the same place when we get back then we know he hasn't been out.'

'*Hi ho, hi ho, it's off to work we go,*' sang Anders, carrying a spade, when a few minutes later they were hurrying along the narrow track up to the ruins.

'If we meet anyone we can say we're digging for worms,' said Kalle.

But they didn't meet anyone, and the ruins stood alone and abandoned as usual. The only sound was the buzzing of bees.

A thought struck Anders.

'How on earth are we going to get into the cellar? You

said that was where the jewellery was, Kalle. How did *you* get in that time you found the pearl?'

This was Kalle's big moment.

'Well, how do you usually get in through locked doors?' he bragged, bringing out the lock pick.

Anders was more impressed than he wanted to admit. 'Holy moly!' he said, and Kalle took that as a compliment.

The door swung open. Now nothing was barring their way, and like a pack of hungry wolves Kalle, Anders and Eva-Lotta bounded down the stairs.

After two hours of digging Anders put down the spade.

'Well, now the cellar floor looks more like a potato allotment. But I've never seen a place with so few diamonds. What a surprise!'

'You can't expect to find them right away,' said Kalle. But he also felt cheated. They had dug every inch of the floor in the large cellar space at the foot of the stairs. This was the actual cellar, but from here many long, dark and partly blocked passages led to crypts, vaults and dungeons. The passages didn't look particularly inviting, but naturally it was possible that Uncle Einar had buried his treasure somewhere deeper in the cellar, to keep it extra safe. They could be digging for a year if they chose to search those tunnels. Assuming he had even hidden them in the ruined castle, that is. Kalle had a growing feeling of doubt.

'Whereabouts did you find the pearl?' asked Eva-Lotta.

'Over there, by the staircase,' said Kalle. 'But we've dug all around there.'

Eva-Lotta sank onto the bottom step, lost in thought. The stone slab at the foot of the stairs was plainly not set firmly into the ground because it wobbled slightly when Eva-Lotta rested her feet on it. Eva-Lotta leapt to her feet.

'You don't possibly imagine . . .' she began, and grabbed the slab eagerly with both hands. 'It's loose, look!'

Two pairs of arms came to her help. The stone slab was shifted aside and a whole army of woodlice scuttled off in all directions.

'Dig here!' said Kalle excitedly to Anders. Anders picked up the spade and thrust it into the ground in the place where the slab had been. It hit something.

'Bound to be a rock,' said Anders, but his hands were shaking slightly as he stuck his fingers down into the earth to feel what it was.

But it wasn't a rock. It was—Anders felt around the object with soil-covered hands—it was a metal box. He lifted it up. It was exactly the same as the one the White Roses had.

Kalle broke the stunned silence.

'The plot thickens,' he said. 'He's stolen our box, the thief.'

Anders shook his head.

'No, it isn't ours. I locked ours with my own hands only a while ago.'

'But it's exactly the same,' said Eva-Lotta.

'Then he must have bought it in the hardware shop at the same time as he bought the torch,' said Kalle. 'The hardware shop is where they sell these boxes.'

'Yes, it's where we got ours from,' said Eva-Lotta.

'Open it, before I have a complete breakdown,' said Kalle.

Anders felt the box. It was locked.

'I wonder if you can use the same key for all these boxes?'

He pulled out the key that was hanging on the piece of string around his neck.

'Oh,' said Eva-Lotta. 'Oh!'

Kalle was breathing as if he had been running a marathon. Anders put in the key and turned it. It worked.

'Oh!' said Eva-Lotta. And when Anders opened the lid: 'Oh, can you believe it! It's exactly like in the *Thousand and One Nights*!'

'Yes, that's just what it looks like. All these emeralds and diamonds!' said Kalle, filled with wonder.

There it all was, exactly as it had been described in

the newspaper: brooches and rings and bracelets and a broken necklace with pearls just like the one Kalle had found.

'A hundred thousand kronor,' whispered Anders. 'It's almost scary.'

Eva-Lotta let the jewellery run through her fingers. She picked up a bracelet and threaded it on her arm, and she pinned a diamond brooch to her blue cotton dress. She put a ring on each and every one of her fingers, and with all her finery went and stood below the narrow window, through which the sunshine was streaming in. She glittered and sparkled.

'Oh, how wonderful! Aren't I like the Queen of Sheba? If only I had at least one tiny weeny little ring!'

'That's women for you,' said Anders.

'We haven't got time for this,' said Kalle. 'We've got to get out of here, fast. Supposing Uncle Einar suddenly hit on the idea of sneaking up here and digging up the box! Supposing he is on his way at this very moment! That would be about as pleasant as bumping into a Bengal tiger.'

'I'd prefer the tiger,' said Anders. 'But you know Uncle Einar doesn't dare go out, because Krok and Redig are watching his every move.'

'Never mind that,' said Kalle. 'We've got to go to the police this instant.'

'The police!' Anders sounded absolutely disgusted.

'You don't mean to say we're getting the police involved just when it's starting to get interesting?'

'It's not exactly the Wars of the Roses, you know,' said Kalle gravely. 'We've got to go to the police now, this very minute. The criminals must be arrested, surely you understand that?'

'Couldn't we lure them into a trap and then say to the police, here you are, three first class rogues that we've captured for you.'

Kalle shook his head. How many times had Master Detective Blomkvist single-handedly dealt with dozens of the very worst criminals! But Master Detective Blomkvist was one person, and Kalle Blomkvist another. And Kalle was a practical and sensible young man.

'Okay then.'

Reluctantly Anders bowed to Kalle's extensive knowledge in the field of crime.

'But in that case,' said Eva-Lotta, 'It's Björk we must tell. Only him and no one else can be allowed to help us. And he might even be made an inspector afterwards.'

Anders studied the result of several hours of digging.

'What are we going to about this lot? Plant potatoes or scrape it all back again?'

Kalle thought it was safest to wipe out any trace of their visit to the cellar.

'But hurry up,' he said. 'It feels stressful sitting here holding a tin box containing a hundred thousand kronor.

I want to get out of here as fast as possible.'

'What shall we do with the box?' asked Eva-Lotta. 'We can't lug it around with us. And where are we going to hide it?'

After some discussion they decided that Anders would take the precious box back to the White Roses' headquarters, while Kalle and Eva-Lotta would look for Constable Björk. Anders took off his shirt and wrapped it round the box. Wearing only his trousers, with the spade in one hand and the wrapped box in the other, he led the return journey.

'I'm sure anyone I bump into will think I've been digging for worms,' he said positively.

Kalle slammed the door behind them and it locked in place.

'It's a pity about one thing,' he said.

'What's that?' asked Eva-Lotta.

'We won't be able to see Uncle Einar's face when he comes to collect the box.'

'Yes, that would be worth a kronor or two,' replied Eva-Lotta.

All was calm and quiet at the police station. An officer was sitting at the desk solving a crossword puzzle, as if there was no crime in the entire world. But it wasn't Björk.

'Is Constable Björk in, please?' asked Kalle politely.

'He is away on police business and won't be back until tomorrow. Can you tell me a mythological monster with eight letters?'

The officer chewed his pencil and looked at Kalle expectantly.

'No. I came here on completely different business,' said Kalle.

'Well, as I said, Björk will be here tomorrow. What about a female warrior, six letters?'

'Eva-Lotta,' said Kalle. 'Oh no, that's eight letters. Well, thanks and goodbye! We'll come back tomorrow.'

Kalle dragged Eva-Lotta onto the street.

'You can't talk about this kind of thing with a cop who's only interested in mythological monsters,' he said.

Eva-Lotta felt the same. They agreed that it probably wouldn't be a risk if they waited until the following day to report their find to the police. After all, Uncle Einar was secure in his bed.

'And there's Krok, outside the watchmaker's,' whispered Kalle to Eva-Lotta. 'Have you ever seen such an ugly hooter in your life?'

'It's nice they keep watch over each other,' said Eva-Lotta. 'As the proverb says: When innocence sleeps, the angels stand guard!'

Kalle flexed his arm muscles.

'But tomorrow, Eva-Lotta, will be a battle of life and death!'

12

The day looked as if was going to be hotter than usual. The lupins in the flower bed in the baker's garden were already drooping. There wasn't a breath of wind and even Tussy preferred to stay in the shade on the veranda, where Frida the maid was busy laying the table for breakfast.

Eva-Lotta came running out in her nightdress and with the mark of the pillow still on her cheek.

'Do you know if Uncle Einar has woken up yet, Frida?'

Frida's face took on a mysterious look.

'You'd be better off asking if he ever went to sleep, because that's just what he didn't do! I can tell you, young Eva-Lotta, that Mr Lindeberg's bed was not slept in last night.'

Eva-Lotta stared at her.

'Frida, what do you mean? How do you know?'

'Well, I went in there to give him his coffee only a minute ago, and the room was empty and his bed the same as it was when I made it yesterday, after he went out. He felt better again towards evening, you see.'

'Did he go out last night after I'd gone to bed?' Eva-Lotta was so eager to know that she gripped Frida's arm.

'I should say so! Probably because of the letter he received. Well I never, I've forgotten the salt and the sugar!'

'A letter? No, Frida, don't go! What letter?'

Eva-Lotta tugged at Frida's arm.

'You're very curious all of a sudden, Eva-Lotta! How do I know what kind of letter it was? I don't read other people's post. But there were two men standing by the gate last night when I went to fetch the milk, and they asked me to give a letter to Mr Lindeberg, which I did, of course. And that put some life into him, I can tell you. And that's all I know!'

It took about a minute for Eva-Lotta to get dressed, and about the same time to rush over to Kalle's. Anders was already there.

'What are we going to do? Uncle Einar has disappeared, and before we had time to arrest him!'

The message was like a dropped bomb.

'I might have known it,' said Anders glumly. 'It feels exactly like when I had that pike on my hook in the spring and it wriggled free at the last minute.'

'Calm down!' urged Kalle—well, in actual fact it was Detective Blomkvist who was paying a guest visit. 'A methodical approach, that's the only way forward. Let us first make a search of Mr Lindeberg's—I mean Uncle Einar's—room.'

As a precaution Kalle went first to check that Krok and Redig weren't standing guard on the pavement. It looks as if the surveillance had ended.

'Bed untouched, suitcase still here,' stated Kalle, after they had crept into Uncle Einar's room. 'It looks as if he's planning to come back. But that could be a bluff, of course.'

Anders and Eva-Lotta sat on the bed looking miserable.

'No, he won't be back,' said Eva-Lotta. 'But at least we've saved the jewels.'

Kalle spun round, his eyes wide. The waste paper basket—of course! Purely routine! Inside were a couple of empty cigarette packets, a few used matches and an old newspaper. And also some tiny, tiny scraps of paper. Kalle whistled.

'Right, we're going to do a jigsaw puzzle,' he said. He collected all the scraps of paper and spread them out on the writing desk. Anders and Eva-Lotta moved in close to see.

'Do you think it can be the letter?' asked Eva-Lotta.

'That's what we're going to find out!'

Kalle moved the pieces around. He fitted together a word here and a word there.

It was the letter. Soon he had completed the puzzle. Three heads leaned expectantly over the desk, and read:

Einar, dear old friend!

We have had a think, me and Matey. Let's split it between us. You've behaved like a swine, it's true, and if we had time we'd get more out of you. But as I said, let's share it. That'll be best for us all, you especially. I hope you understand. But remember, no funny business! Try double-crossing us again and you're not long for this world, I promise you. Play it straight this time! We'll be waiting for you by the gate. Get over here pronto with the sparklers and we'll be gone before you can blink.

Arthur.

'So, the crooks are best buddies again, I see,' said Kalle. 'But they'll have to look hard for the sparklers!'

'I wonder where they are now?' said Anders. 'Could they have left town? I'm guessing they're hopping mad, wherever they are!'

'And won't they wonder who took the jewels!' Eva-Lotta brightened up considerably at that thought.

'What about going to the ruined castle to see if they're still looking? If they are we can tip off the police straight away,' said Anders. Then a thought struck him. 'But how can they get down into the cellar now that Uncle Einar hasn't got his lock pick?'

'Oh, types like Krok and Redig are dripping with lock picks, believe me,' said Kalle. He gathered up the pieces of paper and put them in a cigarette packet, which he then stuffed in his pocket.

'This is evidence, you understand,' he explained to Anders and Eva-Lotta.

It was suffocatingly hot in the sunshine. Anders, Kalle and Eva-Lotta panted. They daren't take the usual path up to the ruins for fear of bumping into the three jewel thieves.

'That really would *not* be a good idea,' said Kalle. 'Then they'd suspect us, and that would be the very worst thing to happen. That Redig doesn't look the sort to be thrilled if someone poked their nose into his business.'

'It's not certain they're still here,' said Anders. 'I think they were scared out of their wits when they saw the jewellery had gone. Unless Uncle Einar has led them on a false trail, of course!'

It was hard work climbing the hill, but it was unavoidable if they weren't going to use the path. They had to hang on to bushes and crawl on their knees and push their way up over rocks. And it was hot, fiendishly hot. Eva-Lotta began to feel hungry. She hadn't had time to eat anything before she left home, but she had put a few bread rolls in her dress pocket.

There were the castle ruins. That was one of the advantages of not taking the path: you came out on a flat piece of ground behind the ruins and could sneak up and peer around the corner to see if there was any danger in sight. But all was quiet. The bees were buzzing as usual, the wild roses had their usual sweet perfume, and the door to the cellar was locked as usual.

'Just as I thought! Vanished! To think we didn't arrest them last night! That will haunt me to my dying day,' said Anders.

'We've got to go down to the cellar to see if they've left any clues,' said Kalle, taking out the lock pick.

'You're handling that lock pick like a natural born thief,' said Anders admiringly, as the door swung open.

All three jostled together down the staircase. At the same time a loud scream filled the old ruins. The person who screamed was Eva-Lotta. And why did she scream? Because someone was lying on the cellar floor. And that someone was Uncle Einar. His hands were tied tightly behind his back and thick rope bound his legs together. And stuffed into his mouth was a handkerchief.

The children's first impulse was to run away. Uncle Einar was their enemy, they knew that. But in his present condition Uncle Einar was completely harmless. He stared at them with bloodshot, pleading eyes. Kalle walked over and freed him from the handkerchief.

Uncle Einar groaned.

'Look what they did to me, the scum! Good grief, my arms! Help me get the rope off!'

Eva-Lotta hurried towards him, but Kalle stopped her.

'One moment,' he said. He looked acutely embarrassed.

'Excuse us, Uncle Einar, but we have to go to the police first.' He thought it was absolutely extraordinary that he dared to say such a thing to an adult.

Uncle Einar let out a stream of obscenities. Then he groaned again.

'Ah I see, it's you I have to thank for this pleasure! I should have realized. Master Detective Kalle Blomkvist!'

It was unpleasant listening to his groaning.

'And you can blasted well leave off gawking at me like that!' he shouted. 'Go and get the police then, you snotty-nosed brats! But you could at least give me some water!'

Anders ran as fast as he could up to the spring in the courtyard. There was clear, fresh water in the basin and a large iron ladle to drink from.

When Anders lifted the ladle to Uncle Einar's mouth he drank as if he had never seen water before. Then he started groaning again.

'Oh, my arms!'

It was more than Kalle could stand.

'If you promise not to try and escape we could loosen the rope a little.'

'I'll promise whatever you ask,' said Uncle Einar.

'And anyway, it isn't worth trying because if one of us runs to the police there are at least two of us left to guard you. And your legs are tied as well.'

'Your powers of observation are to be greatly admired,' said Uncle Einar.

Anders managed, not without difficulty, to untie the rope holding Uncle Einar's arms behind his back. When the rope came loose the pain was clearly worse than ever, because Uncle Einar rocked backwards and forwards for a long while, moaning.

'How long have you been lying here like this, Uncle Einar?' asked Eva-Lotta. Her voice was shaking.

'Since last night, my dear young lady,' said Uncle Einar. 'All thanks to your interference.'

'Yes, that's a pity,' said Kalle. 'And now, if you'll excuse me, we must go for the police!'

'Can't we discuss the situation?' asked Uncle Einar. 'And what the dickens have you been up to, snooping into my affairs? Whatever else, it's plainly you who have taken the jewels, and the most important thing is that they're safe, Mr Detective. Can't you let a poor old offender go free, for friendship's sake?'

The children kept silent.

'Eva-Lotta,' begged Uncle Einar. 'You don't want relations of yours ending up in jail, do you?'

'When you've done something wrong then you must take your punishment,' said Eva-Lotta.

'I think it's the only thing we can do,' said Kalle. 'Anders, will you go?'

'Yes,' said Anders.

'Wretched children!' bellowed Uncle Einar. 'If only I had wrung your necks when I had the chance!'

Anders leapt up the stairs in a couple of bounds. Now all he had to do was rush out of the door. But—there was something blocking his path. Two things, to be precise, standing in the doorway. One of them was the pale-faced man, and he was holding a pistol.

13

'Seems we have arrived in the middle of a family get-together,' laughed Pale Face. 'Uncle Einar, surrounded by his nearest and dearest! How touching. We ought to take a photo and send it to the newspaper. Don't misunderstand me, Einar old chap, I don't mean the Police Times. There are other publications!'

He paused and studied his pistol.

'Such a pity we came and interrupted you,' he went on. 'If we had turned up any later your little friends would have let you go, and that might have made it easier for you to find the sparklers than last night.'

'Arthur, listen to me a minute,' said Uncle Einar. I swear . . .'

'You did enough of that last night,' Pale Face interrupted him. 'When you feel you want to tell us what you have done with the goods, then you can open your mouth. Until then, keep your trap shut! And until then you can stay there like a stranded whale. I hope your little friends have got nothing against us tying your arms again? And you're not too hungry or thirsty are you, old chap, because unfortunately I can't give you anything except this handkerchief to chew on. Until you have come to your senses, that is!'

'Arthur!' Uncle Einar called out in desperation. 'You've got to listen to what I'm saying! Do you know who's got their grubby hands on it? These little tykes here!' He pointed at the children. 'And they were on their way to get the cops when you burst in. Blimey, I never thought I'd be able to say I was pleased to see you and Matey, but you turned up as if I'd sent for you.'

There was a short silence. The pale face with its nervous eyes turned to face the children. Kalle felt a presentiment of colossal danger. This was something different and much worse than when he had faced Uncle Einar's pistol.

Nasty, whose name was obviously Matey, broke the silence.

'Perhaps he's speaking the truth for once, Arthur?'

'Possibly,' replied Arthur. 'We'll soon find out.'

'Let me take care of the brats,' said Uncle Einar. 'I'll soon find out what I need to know.'

Anders, Kalle and Eva-Lotta's faces turned a shade whiter. Kalle was right. This certainly was something different from the Wars of the Roses.

'Arthur,' said Uncle Einar. 'If you've finally got it into your head that I won't try to trick you any more, then you must see that we've got to stick together, now more than ever. Cut this'—he pointed to the rope around his legs—'and let's get organized. I have a feeling it's high time we got out of here!'

Without a word Arthur walked up and cut the rope. Uncle Einar stood up with difficulty and rubbed his aching limbs.

'That was the longest night I've ever experienced in my entire life,' he said.

His friend Arthur smiled a menacing smile, and Matey laughed scornfully.

Uncle Einar sidled over to Kalle and grabbed his chin.

'What do you say now, Mr Detective? Weren't you going to send for the police?'

Kalle didn't answer. The game was over, and he knew it.

'I can tell you, Arthur,' continued Uncle Einar. 'These children are unbelievably sensible. It wouldn't surprise me if they very kindly told Uncle Einar where they have hidden the jewellery they sniffed out.'

'We haven't got it here, and we're not telling you where it is,' declared Anders.

'Listen to me a second, kids,' said Uncle Einar. 'These two very nice gents you see here got things a bit muddled up yesterday. They had the idea I knew where the jewels were hidden and didn't want to tell them. And so they gave me a night to think it over. And as I just said, it was the longest night I've ever known. It's pretty dark down here in the cellar at night. Pitch black in fact, and cold. And you sleep very badly when your arms are tied behind your back, I can tell you that. It's much nicer sleeping at your mum's house, isn't it, Eva-Lotta?'

Eva-Lotta looked at Uncle Einar with the same expression as the day he had tormented her beloved Tussy.

'Master Detective,' Uncle Einar continued. 'How would you like to spend one or shall we say a couple of nights here in the ruins? Or rather, all your remaining nights?'

Kalle felt a small, unpleasant sense of fear trickle down his backbone.

'We're in a hurry,' interrupted Arthur Redig. 'This nonsense has gone on far too long. Listen here, kids! I love children, I really do, but brats who get it into their heads to run to the police all the time, those I don't like. We are going to lock you in this cellar, we have no choice. But it depends on you whether you get out alive. Produce the goods and you won't have to stay here more than a night or two. As soon as we are safe, your kind Uncle Einar will write to say where you are.'

He paused.

'Or if you *don't* want to tell us where you have hidden the jewellery, well, it will be so pitiful for your mothers that I don't dare think about it.'

Anders and Kalle and Eva-Lotta didn't dare think about

it either. Kalle gave the other two a questioning look and Eva-Lotta and Anders nodded in agreement. What else could they do? They had to reveal the whereabouts of the tin box.

'Well, Mr Detective?' asked Uncle Einar encouragingly.

'Do you promise you'll let us out if we tell you?' asked Kalle.

'By all means,' replied Uncle Einar. 'Don't you trust Uncle Einar, lad? You'll only have to stay here until we've found a more congenial place than this town. And I'll even ask Uncle Arthur here not to tie you up, so you'll be nice and comfortable.'

'The tin box is in the white chest of drawers in the bakery loft,' said Kalle, and it looked like an enormous effort for him to get the words out. 'Where we had our Circus Kalott.'

'Splendid,' said Uncle Einar.

'Are you sure you know where it is, Einar?' asked Arthur Redig.

'Absolutely! And now you see, Arthur, why it's best for us to stick together. Neither of you can go up into the bakery loft without attracting attention, but I can.'

'All right!' said Arthur. 'Let's get going.'

He looked at the three children standing silently side by side.

'I hope you've told us the truth! Honesty is the best policy, my young friends. That proverb will get you far in this life. If you've lied to us we'll be back very soon, and oh dear, what a shame that will be. What a shame!'

'We haven't lied,' said Kalle, glaring angrily from under his fringe.

Uncle Einar walked up to him, but Kalle refused to shake his outstretched hand.

'Farewell, Master Detective,' he said. 'I guess it will be wisest to shelve your sleuthing in future. And while we're at it, can I have my lock pick back? It was you who took it, am I right?'

Kalle pushed his hand into his pocket and brought out the lock pick.

'There are one or two things Uncle Einar would be wise to shelve as well,' he said grimly. Uncle Einar laughed.

'Bye bye, Anders, nice to have met you! Bye, Eva-Lotta! Such a sweet child, I always thought. Say goodbye from me to your mother, in case I don't have time to do it myself!'

He climbed the stairs accompanied by his two partners. In the doorway he turned and waved.

'I promise I'll write and tell them where you are—assuming I can remember!'

The heavy door slammed shut behind them.

14

'It's all my fault,' said Kalle, after what seemed like an endless silence. 'It is absolutely my fault. I shouldn't have got you mixed up in this. And maybe not myself, either.'

'What do you mean, your fault?' said Eva-Lotta. 'You never dreamed it would turn out like this.'

It went silent again, a very unpleasant silence. It was as if the outside world no longer existed. All that remained was this cellar and the firmly locked door.

'What a shame Björk wasn't around yesterday,' said Anders eventually.

'You can say that again,' said Kalle.

Then no one spoke for a while. They were thinking. And probably all three were thinking the same thing. It had been a failure. The jewellery was gone, the thieves would escape abroad. But at that precise moment it was nothing compared to the fact that they were imprisoned here with no means of getting out or knowing if they ever would get out. They could not follow that horrific thought to its logical conclusion. What if Uncle Einar didn't bother writing? And, by the way, how long did it take for a letter to come from abroad? How long could you survive without food and drink? And wasn't it best for the robbers if the children stayed down here in the cellar for ever? There were police in other countries too, of course, and if the children revealed who the culprits were, Uncle Einar and his partners in crime wouldn't be as secure as they would if Kalle, Anders and Eva-Lotta had no opportunity to reveal their names. 'I'll write—assuming I can remember.' That was the last thing Uncle Einar had said, and it sounded ominous.

'I've got three rolls,' said Eva-Lotta, and thrust her hand into the pocket of her dress.

That was a small comfort, at least.

'Then we won't die of starvation until later this afternoon,' said Anders. 'We've got half a ladle of water left, too.'

Three rolls and half a ladle of water! And then what?

'We must shout for help,' said Kalle. 'Perhaps a tourist will come along to look at the ruins.'

'I seem to recall there were two tourists last summer,' said Anders. 'People in the town talked about it for ages afterwards. So why shouldn't there be one today?'

They went and stood below the tiny gap that was the cellar window. A ray of sunlight was streaming in.

'One, two, three—now!' commanded Anders.

'Help! H-ee-ee-lp!'

The following silence was denser than ever.

'They can go and visit other castles,' said Anders bitterly. 'But no one cares about this one.'

No, no tourists ran to answer their call for help, and no one else either.

The minutes passed and then became hours.

'If only I had told them at home I was going to the ruins,' said Eva-Lotta. 'They would have come looking for us sooner or later.'

She buried her head in her hands. Kalle gulped a few times and got up from the floor. It was unbearable sitting there watching Eva-Lotta like that. What about the door—was there any way they could break it down? It only took a look to confirm that any attempt would be useless. Kalle bent over to pick up something from the ground. It was Uncle Einar's torch. Imagine that—he had forgotten it! What luck! Soon it would be night, dark cold night. It was comforting to know they could banish the darkness for a while if they needed to. Naturally a battery wouldn't last forever, but they could at least turn it on to see what the time was. Not that it actually mattered whether it was three or four or five—soon nothing would matter. Kalle felt a dull despair rise up inside him. He trudged around 'prey to gloomy thoughts', as it always says in books. But anything was better than sitting and waiting. Everything was better. It would even be better to investigate the dark maze of tunnels that led into the inner regions of the cellar.

'Anders, you said once you wanted to explore the whole cellar, to map it out and make it our headquarters. Why not make the most of it and do it now?'

'Did I really say anything so stupid? I must have had sunstroke that day. If ever I get out of here, I know one person who's never going to set foot anywhere near these rotten old ruins again, trust me!'

'But I still wonder where those tunnels go,' persisted Kalle. 'What if there's another way out that no one knows about?'

'And what if a whole gang of archaeologists turn up and dig us out this afternoon. That's just about as realistic.'

Eva-Lotta leapt to her feet.

'But if we sit here we'll go crackers in no time,' she said. 'I think we should do as Kalle says. We've got the torch, haven't we? That'll show us the way.'

'Fair enough,' said Anders. 'But shall we eat first? Three rolls are three rolls, whatever we end up doing.'

Eva-Lotta gave them one bread roll each and they ate in silence. It felt weird and very scary to think this might be the last time they ate anything in this life. They washed the rolls down with the water that was left in the ladle. Then they held hands and set off on their journey into the darkness. Kalle went first, lighting their way with the torch.

At that precise moment a car pulled up outside the little town's police station. Two men jumped out—two police officers. They hurried into the police station where they were met by Constable Björk. He looked rather astonished at the unexpected visit. The two men introduced themselves.

'Detective Superintendent Stenberg, Detective Inspector Santesson, Stockholm Criminal Investigation Unit.'

Then the detective superintendent went on briskly:

'Constable, are you familiar with a private detective by the name of Blomkvist in this town?'

'Private Detective Blomkvist?' Constable Björk shook his head. 'Never heard of him!'

'That's odd,' continued the detective inspector. 'He lives at 14 High Street. See for yourself.'

The detective superintendent slid a letter over to Björk. If Kalle had been there he would have recognized it.

To the Criminal Investigation Unit, Stockholm Police was written at the top. And sure enough, it was signed by *Karl Blomkvist, Private detective.*

Constable Björk began to laugh.

'That can be none other than my friend Kalle Blomkvist. Private detective, I ask you! He's about twelve or thirteen years old, our private detective.'

'Listen, man, how do you explain the fact that he has sent us a fingerprint which exactly matches the ones we collected at the Östermalm break-in at the end of June? You know, that major jewellery heist! And who does this fingerprint belong to? That is what the Criminal Investigation Unit in Stockholm would dearly like to know! It is in fact the only lead we have. We are convinced there must have been several people involved to be able to shift that heavy safe, but only one of them left any fingerprints. The others evidently wore gloves.'

Constable Björk sat down to have a think. He recalled Kalle's question when they had met on the High Street the other day: '*What do you do if you know a person is a crook, but you can't prove it?*' However he had done it, Kalle had evidently tracked down the perpetrators of the huge jewellery robbery.

'The only way to proceed is to ask Kalle ourselves,' said Constable Björk.

'Yes, and let's make it snappy,' said the detective superintendent.

'14, High Street,' said the detective inspector, and got behind the wheel.

And away swept the police car.

The Red Roses were unbearably bored. The Whites had offered unconditional surrender just when the feud was starting to look promising—what kind of behaviour was that? What on earth were they thinking of, backing out of such good fun of their own free will?

'I think we'll pay them a visit and tell them what we think of them,' said Sixten. 'Then maybe they'll come to their senses.'

Benka and Jonte thought that was a good suggestion.

But the Whites' headquarters was silent and abandoned.

'Where do you suppose they can be?' asked Jonte.

'We'll wait for them to return,' said Sixten. 'They're sure to be back at some stage.'

At which point the Reds installed themselves comfortably in the bakery loft. There was a heap of old comics, which helped the Whites pass the time when the weather was bad. There was also a game of Ludo and, of course, that excellent table where you could play ping-pong. So there was no lack of things to do.

'Brilliant headquarters the Whites have got here,' said Benka.

'Yep,' said Sixten. 'I wish there was room for a ping-pong table in my garage.'

They played table tennis and in between matches slid down the rope and climbed up again, and read comics, and weren't at all bothered that the Whites weren't there.

Sixten stood in the hatch and held the rope. Oh look, here comes that creep who was Eva-Lotta's relation, whatever his name was. Yes—Uncle Einar. Cripes, he's in a hurry, thought Sixten. Then Uncle Einar looked up and saw Sixten, and stopped.

'Are you looking for Eva-Lotta?' he said, after a moment.

'Yes,' replied Sixten. 'Do you happen to know where she is?'

'No,' said Uncle Einar. 'I don't.'

'Right,' said Sixten, and he swished down the rope. Uncle Einar's face lit up.

Sixten started climbing back up.

'You're going up again, then?' asked Uncle Einar.

'Yep,' said Sixten, climbing even faster. He was a very good gymnast, you could tell.

'What are you doing up there?' asked Uncle Einar.

'Waiting for Eva-Lotta,' said Sixten.

Uncle Einar paced up and down.

'When I come to think of it,' he called to Sixten, 'I recall Eva-Lotta saying she and the lads were going on an outing today. They're not due back until late this evening.'

'Oh, right,' said Sixten, and he slid down the rope again. Uncle Einar looked happy.

Sixten grabbed hold of the rope and began to clamber up.

'Didn't you hear what I said?' Uncle Einar said impatiently. 'Eva-Lotta won't be back all day.'

'Yep,' said Sixten. 'That's a shame.'

He carried on climbing.

'What are you going to do up there now?' called Uncle Einar.

'Read Mandrake the Magician comics,' said Sixten.

Now Uncle Einar didn't look at all happy. He walked rapidly up and down.

'Hello, you up there,' he shouted after a while. 'Do you want to earn a few kronor?'

Sixten stuck his head through the hatch.

'Yes! How do I do that?'

'Run to the tobacconist's and buy me a packet of Lucky Strike!'

'Okay,' said Sixten, and he swooshed down the rope again. Uncle Einar gave him some money and Sixten shot off. Uncle Einar looked happier than ever.

Now Benka stuck his head out through the hatch, sturdy little Benka with his mop of curly blonde hair and his upturned nose. There was no reason to swear at such a cheery little fellow, but that's exactly what Uncle Einar did. At length.

After a few minutes Sixten returned. In one hand he had a large bag. He gave the cigarettes to Uncle Einar and then called up to the Reds.

'Look, I've bought cakes from Eva-Lotta's dad, and

he's always been a generous man. Now we've got food to last all day and we won't have to go home.'

Then Uncle Einar swore silently to himself for even longer than before, and strode off.

The Reds read Mandrake the Magician comics and played table tennis and ate cakes and swooshed down the rope, and it really didn't bother them that the Whites weren't there.

15

Darkness, darkness everywhere! From time to time faint streams of light make their way through tiny openings in the wall. But at least the torch is still working, and it is certainly needed. It's hard for them to make their way forwards. Sometimes there are huge boulders blocking the way. It's damp, slippery and cold. Imagine spending the night here! Many nights!

Anders and Kalle and Eva-Lotta hold hands. Kalle shines the light along the stone walls, where water seeped in.

'Think of those poor souls who were locked up in here in the old days,' says Eva-Lotta. 'Perhaps for many years!'

'But at least they had food,' grumbles Anders. One small bread roll wasn't exactly filling, and he is very hungry. 'We usually have dinner at home about this time!'

'We were having meatballs today,' says Eva-Lotta, and sighs.

Kalle keeps quiet. He walks along feeling angry with

himself for even thinking about getting involved in that stupid detective work. They could have been sitting in the bakery loft now, fighting the Reds, cycling and swimming and eating meatballs for dinner, and doing all sorts of other things. Instead, here they are, trudging along miserably in the dark, not even daring to think what might happen.

'I think it's best we go back to our starting point now,' says Eva-Lotta. 'We've probably seen all there is to see, and it's the same all the way along, just as dark and horrible everywhere.'

'Let's at least follow this passage to the end,' suggests Anders. 'Then we can turn back.'

Eva-Lotta was wrong. It isn't exactly the same everywhere. This passage ends in a staircase, and a staircase means a link between two floors. It is a narrow, spiral staircase, where the stones have been worn down by many feet. Anders and Kalle and Eva-Lotta stand absolutely still. They can't believe their eyes. Kalle directs the torch ahead and then he rushes up the stairs. But the staircase is boarded shut at the top to stop anyone getting into the cellar. Or getting out of it, either. Kalle feels like barging his head right through the wood and making the splinters fly.

'We've got to get out! We've *got* to get out, I tell you!' Anders sounds wild. 'I can't stand it a minute longer!'

He grabs hold of a large rock. Kalle helps him.

'One, two, three—now!' Anders orders. The wood cracks. 'Do it again! It'll work, you'll see, Kalle!' Anders is almost sobbing with excitement.

One final time with all their strength. Crash! Pieces of wood shoot in all directions. It's easy to move them out of the way. Anders climbs through and gives a yelp of joy. The stairs lead up to the castle's ground floor.

'Come on, Kalle and Eva-Lotta,' he yells.

But Kalle and Eva-Lotta are already there. They all stare at the daylight, at the sunshine, as if it is a miracle. Eva-Lotta rushes over to a window. Down there is the little town. She can see the river and the water tower and the church. And there, far away, she can see the red roof of the bakery. Then she leans against the stone wall and bursts into loud sobs.

Girls are certainly strange, think Kalle and Anders. Before, down in the cellar, she didn't cry at all, but now, when all danger is over, the tears are spurting out like a fountain.

By this time the Reds have read all the Mandrake comics and they simply can't play another game of ping-pong. And anyway, there's going to be a football match on the Prairie soon.

'Let's not wait any longer,' says Sixten. 'They must have emigrated to America. Come on, let's get out of here.'

They slide down the rope, Sixten, Benka and Jonte, and charge over the river on Eva-Lotta's bridge. And so Uncle Einar finally gets the opportunity he has waited several hours for.

A black Volvo is parked on the street a few hundred metres further on. Two men are sitting inside, two anxious and impatient men. They have been sitting there in the heat for such a long time. The hours have crawled by, and every so often their old chum Einar has returned with an update:

'The brats are still there! Well, what do you want me to do! I can't wring their necks, however much I feel tempted.'

But here comes Einar at last, practically jogging. He is carrying something under his jacket.

'All done,' he whispers, and jumps in.

Matey presses the accelerator and the Volvo shoots off at top speed, heading north out of the town.

The three men in the car have no other thought than to leave the little town behind them as quickly as they can. They are looking straight ahead. They see only the road that will carry them to riches and freedom and independence. If they had glanced to one side they would have seen three children, Anders, Kalle and Eva-

Lotta, appear round the street corner and with surprise and horror watch their enemies disappearing.

16

'You tiresome boy, where have you been?' said Mr Blomkvist the grocer. 'And what have you done? Have you been breaking windows again?'

For the hundredth time the grocer had gone out on to the shop's front step to see if there was any sign of his offspring. And at last he had caught sight of him at the street corner with Anders and Eva-Lotta.

'Let me go, Dad!' shouted Kalle. 'I've got to see the police right away!'

'I know,' said his father. 'The police are at home, waiting for you. Things don't look good for you, Kalle.'

Kalle hadn't the faintest idea why the police were waiting for him, but it was enough for him that they were. He ran as he had never run in his life. Anders and Eva-Lotta rocketed after him.

There was Constable Björk, sitting on the green see-saw, God bless him, and beside him stood two other police officers.

'Arrest them, arrest them!' Kalle yelled frantically.

'Hurry!'

Björk and the two other men hurried up to him.

'The jewellery thieves!' Kalle was in such a state that he could hardly get the words out. 'They've just driven off! Quick!'

He didn't have to say it twice. Mr Blomkvist came lumbering down the road just in time to see Kalle and his two friends being bundled inside the police car with three policemen right behind them. Mr Blomkvist slapped his forehead. His son, taken into custody at such a young age! It was shocking. The only comfort was that the baker's daughter was just as bad. And so was the shoemaker's lad, for that matter!

The police car headed north at such breakneck speed it made the law-abiding citizens of the small town shake their heads. Kalle, Anders and Eva-Lotta sat in the back seat alongside Detective Superintendent Stenberg. They were thrown from side to side as the car swerved. Eva-Lotta wondered how much you could put up with in one day without fainting. Kalle and Anders jabbered away until the superintendent said he could only listen to one at a time. Kalle waved his arms about and shrieked:

'One of them is pale-looking, one looks really creepy, and one is Uncle Einar, but the pale one is actually creepier than the creepy one. Uncle Einar's pretty creepy too. Pale Face calls himself Ivar Redig but in actual fact he's called Arthur, and they call the ugly one Matey, but his name might be Krok, and Uncle Einar is called Lindeberg *and* Brane, and he sleeps with a pistol under his pillow and he buried the jewellery in the castle ruins at the bottom of the stairs, and when I took his fingerprint I knocked the flower pot down, unlucky, eh?, and then he aimed the pistol at me, and then I sat in the maple tree and heard Matey and Redig threaten to kill him, and then they tied him up in the castle cellar because he was stupid enough to take them there, because by that time the jewellery had gone, because we had it hidden in the bakery loft, but unfortunately they've taken it now because they locked us in the cellar and boy, there are so many tunnels down there. But we got out and, well, now you know all of it, but *please* drive faster!'

The detective superintendent didn't look as if he knew all of it, but he reckoned he could save all the details for later.

The detective inspector looked at the speedometer. They were up to sixty-five miles an hour now and he daren't go any faster, even though Kalle thought it was taking far too long.

'Fork in the road, Superintendent. Shall we go left or right?'

The inspector braked the car so abruptly it skidded.

Anders and Kalle and Eva-Lotta were nervously chewing their fingers at this delay.

'What a nuisance,' said the superintendent. 'Constable

Björk, you know the roads around here. Which way do you think they went?'

'Impossible to say,' said Björk. 'They can reach the motorway whichever road they choose.'

'Just a minute,' said Kalle, and he stepped out of the car. He pulled his notebook from his pocket and ran over to road that turned left. He scrutinized the ground closely.

'They drove this way!' he yelled excitedly.

Björk and the superintendent had also got out of the car.

'How do you know that?' asked the superintendent.

'Well, the car has got a special kind of tyre on the rear near-side wheel, and I drew the pattern of the tread in my notebook. And look here!'

He pointed at a clear imprint on the gravelly road surface.

'Identical!'

'You're a bright lad and no mistake,' said the superintendent, as they raced back to the car.

'Oh, purely routine,' said Master Detective Blomkvist. But then he remembered that he would really rather be plain old Kalle. 'It was just an idea I had,' he added modestly.

Their speed was now almost deadly. No one spoke. Everyone's eyes were staring through the windscreen. They skidded round a curve in the road.

'There!' shouted Constable Björk. A hundred metres in front of them was a car.

'That's the one!' said Kalle. 'A black Volvo.'

Detective Inspector Santesson did his utmost to drive faster, but the black Volvo sped on and kept its lead. A face peered out of the rear window. It was clear they had realized they were being followed.

I'm going to faint any second, thought Eva-Lotta. And I've never fainted before.

Seventy miles an hour. Now the police car was slowly but surely catching up with the black Volvo.

'Get down, kids!' yelled the superintendent suddenly. 'They're shooting!'

He shoved all three children down to the floor. It was just in time. A bullet came whistling through the windscreen.

'Björk, you're in the best position. Take my pistol and give those thugs a taste of their own medicine.'

The superintended handed his pistol to his colleague in the front seat.

'They're shooting. Yikes, they're really shooting,' whispered Kalle from the car floor.

Constable Björk opened the side window and stuck out his arm. Not only was he a good gymnast, he was also an excellent sharpshooter. He aimed carefully at the Volvo's rear right-hand tyre. They were no more than twenty-five metres away by this time. He fired, and a split second later the black Volvo skidded and went down into the ditch. The police car drew up alongside.

'Quick, before they have time to get out of the motor,' cried the superintendent. 'You kids stay where you are!'

Within a few seconds the police officers had surrounded the car in the ditch. Nothing in the world would have kept Kalle on the floor of the police car. He had to get up and look.

'Constable Björk and that detective who was driving are pointing their guns,' he reported to Anders and Eva-Lotta. 'And that fat superintendent is yanking open the car door. Oh, what a punch-up! There's Redig, he's got his pistol as well. Whack, Björk just thumped him so he dropped his gun, oh, brilliant, and there's Uncle Einar, but he hasn't got a gun, he's just fighting, but now, you'll never guess, they're putting handcuffs on that villain, and on Redig too. But where's Matey? Oh, they're dragging him out. Looks like he's passed out. This is so exciting! And now, would you believe . . .'

'Give it a rest,' said Anders. 'We've got eyes in our heads, we can see for ourselves.'

The skirmish was over. There facing the superintendent were Uncle Einar and Pale Face. Matey lay on the ground at their feet.

'Well, well,' said the superintendent. 'If it isn't Arthur Berg. What a pleasant surprise.'

'The pleasure is definitely all yours,' said Pale Face,

with a nasty look in his eye.

'I quite agree,' said the superintendent. 'What do you say about that, Santesson? We've nabbed Arthur Berg.'

You've got to have a good memory to remember all the names, thought Kalle.

'Hey, Kalle!' called the superintendent. 'Come here a minute! It might amuse you to hear that thanks to you we have caught one of the most dangerous criminals in the country.'

Even Arthur Berg raised his eyebrows when he saw Kalle and Anders and Eva-Lotta.

'I should have followed my first instinct and shot them there and then,' he said calmly. 'It never pays to be kind to people, it only brings trouble.'

Matey opened his eyes.

'And here we have yet another old acquaintance and regular customer of ours! Well, Matey, didn't you tell me last time we met that you were going straight?'

'I did,' said Matey. 'But I thought I'd get a little start-up money first. It costs money to go straight, superintendent.'

'And as for you.' The superintendent turned to Uncle Einar. 'Is this the first time you've been led astray?'

'Yes,' he said. Then he looked angrily at Kalle. 'At least, I haven't been caught before! And I would have got away with it this time, too, if it hadn't been for Master Detective Blomkvist over there.'

He forced his mouth into a most unfriendly smile.

'And now let's see where we have the loot. Santesson, search the car. I assume it's inside.'

Yes, there it was. The tin box!

'Which of you has the key?' asked the superintendent.

Grudgingly Uncle Einar held it out. Everyone was looking on expectantly.

'Now we'll see,' said the superintendent. He turned the key and lifted the lid.

On the top was a sheet of paper. *Private Documents Belonging to the White Roses*, it said in large letters. The superintendent gazed in amazement. So did the others, not least Uncle Einar and his two companions. Arthur Berg gave Uncle Einar a look full of hate.

The superintendent rummaged through the box. Inside was nothing but sheets of paper and pebbles and some other useless objects.

Eva-Lotta was the first to start giggling—a loud, mischievous giggle. That was the signal for Kalle and Anders. The laughter bubbled up inside them. They laughed, oh, how they laughed, until they doubled over, all three of them, and held their stomachs. They laughed so much they made themselves choke.

'What in the world has got into those children,' said the superintendent, puzzled. Then he turned to Arthur Berg.

'So, you've already manged to stash away the haul. But

we'll get it out of you, don't you worry.'

'You . . . you . . . don't need to get it out of them,' Anders managed to say, as he hiccupped with laughter. 'I know where it is. It's in the bottom drawer, up in the bakery loft.'

'But where did they get that from?' asked the superintendent, pointing at the tin box.

'The top drawer!'

Eva-Lotta suddenly stopped laughing and sank in a heap at the roadside.

'I do believe the young lady has fainted,' said Constable Björk, and he lifted up Eva-Lotta. 'And that's not so surprising.'

Then Eva-Lotta opened her eyes, with some difficulty.

'No, not surprising at all,' she whispered. 'Seeing as I've only eaten one bread roll.'

17

Master Detective Blomkvist lay on his back under the pear tree. Yes, he really was a master detective now, and not plain old Kalle. It was even in the paper, the one he was holding in his hand. '*Master Detective Blomkvist*,' read the headline, and underneath was his photograph. It was true, the photo didn't show the mature man with chiselled features and a piercing gaze you might expect. The face that stared out of the newspaper was remarkably Kalle-like, but that couldn't be helped. Anders and Eva-Lotta's pictures were there too, but a little further down the column.

'Have you noticed, young man?' Mr Blomkvist said to his imaginary listener, 'The entire front page is all about that little case of the stolen jewellery I managed to solve the other day, when I had a spare moment.'

Oh yes, his imaginary listener had indeed noticed, and he couldn't express his admiration strongly enough.

'I'm sure you were very well-rewarded, Mr Blomkvist, sir,' he said.

'I don't know about that,' said Mr Blomkvist. 'Naturally I got a massive amount of dosh—I mean, I received a not inconsiderable sum of money, but I shared it with Miss Lisander and Mr Bengtsson, who were more than a little help to me in my detective work. Truth to tell, we shared ten thousand kronor, which bank manager Östberg is looking after for us.'

His imaginary listener clapped his hands in astonishment.

Mr Blomkvist, with a superior expression, snapped off a blade of grass. 'Ten thousand kronor certainly is a lot of money, but I can tell you, young man, I do not work for gold alone. I have one single goal—to tackle crime in our society. Hercule Poirot, Lord Peter Wimsey and yours truly—yes there are still a few of us left who refuse to allow criminality to get the upper hand.'

The imaginary listener readily agreed that society owed a great debt to Messer's Poirot, Wimsey and Blomkvist for their selfless work in the pursuit of good.

'Before we go our separate ways, young man,' said the master detective, taking the pipe from his mouth, 'there is something I want to say to you. Crime doesn't pay! Honesty goes a long way, even Arthur Berg said that to me once. And I hope he realizes it, wherever he finds himself now. In any case, he has many years ahead of him to work it out. And Uncle Einar, would you believe it. Einar Lindeberg, such a young man and already a career in crime! May his punishment make him change his ways for the better! Because—as I always say—crime doesn't pay!'

'Kalle!'

Eva-Lotta stuck her head through the gap in the fence.

'Kalle, what are you doing there, staring into space? Come over to me instead! Anders and I are going into town.'

'Goodbye, young man,' said Master Detective Blomkvist. 'Miss Lisander has called me and, incidentally, she is the young lady I intend to marry.'

His imaginary listener wished Miss Lisander all the best in her choice of husband.

'Yes, well, Miss Lisander doesn't know it yet,' said the master detective truthfully, and hopped over to the fence, where the aforementioned young lady and Mr Bengtsson were waiting for him.

It was Saturday evening. Peace reigned as Kalle, Anders and Eva-Lotta came strolling down the High Street. The chestnut tree flowers had disappeared long since, but the small gardens were full of roses and lupins and snapdragons. They took the path down towards the carpenter's workshop. Fredrik the Foot was already drunk and waiting for Constable Björk. Kalle, Anders and Eva-Lotta lingered a while to hear Fredrik tell a few stories about his life. Then they wandered on towards the Prairie.

'Look, there's Sixten, Benka and Jonte,' Anders said suddenly, and a gleam came into his eyes. Kalle and Eva-Lotta moved closer to their leader and they marched straight up to the Reds.

They met, and according to the peace treaty the leader of the Whites now had to bow three times to the Reds and say: 'I know I am not worthy to tread the same ground as you, oh master!' The Reds' leader looked expectantly at the Whites' leader, who opened his mouth and said:

'Weedy little squirts!'

The leader of the Reds looked very satisfied. At the same time he took an indignant step backwards.

'This means war,' he said.

'Yes,' said the Whites' leader, and thumped his chest dramatically. 'War is now declared between the Red Roses and the White Roses, and it shall send a thousand souls to death and deadly night!'

ALSO BY ASTRID LINDGREN

A Kalle Blomkvist Mystery:
The White Rose Rescue

A Kalle Blomkvist Mystery:
Living Dangerously

Seacrow Island

Mio's Kingdom

Ronia the Robber's Daughter

Pippi Longstocking
Pippi Longstocking Goes Aboard
Pippi Longstocking in the South Seas

Karlson on the Roof
Karlson Flies Again
The World's Best Karlson

Emil's Clever Pig
Emil and the Great Escape
Emil and the Sneaky Rat

Lotta Says 'No!'
Lotta Makes a Mess

The Children of Noisy Village
Happy Times in Noisy Village
Nothing But Fun in Noisy Village

Astrid Lindgren

Astrid Lindgren was born in Vimmerby, Sweden in 1907. In the course of her life she wrote over 40 books for children, and has sold over 145 million copies worldwide. She once commented, 'I write to amuse the child within me, and can only hope that other children may have some fun that way too.'

Many of Astrid Lindgren's stories are based upon her memories of childhood and they are filled with lively and unconventional characters. Perhaps the best known is Pippi Longstocking, first published in Sweden in 1945. It was an immediate success, and was published in England in 1954.

Awards for Astrid Lindgren's writing include the prestigious Hans Christian Andersen Award. In 1989 a theme park dedicated to her—*Astrid Lindgren Värld* (Astrid Lindgren World)—was opened in Vimmerby. She died in 2002 at the age of 94.

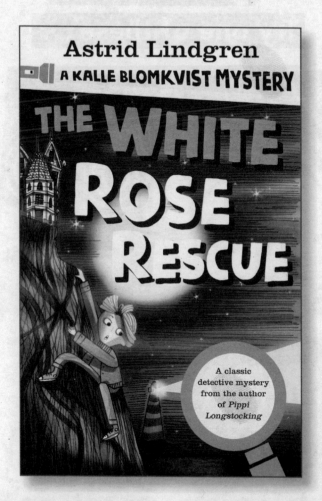

Astrid Lindgren

A KALLE BLOMKVIST MYSTERY

THE WHITE ROSE RESCUE

A classic detective mystery from the author of *Pippi Longstocking*

When Kalle Blomkvist becomes an eye-witness to a mysterious kidnapping he doesn't hesitate to take on the case, one which becomes his most dangerous and challenging yet.

Ready for more great stories?
Try one of these ...

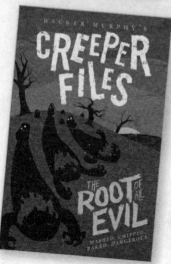